MY HEART

ELSE LASKER-SCHÜLER

MY HEART

A NOVEL OF LOVE, WITH PICTURES AND REAL, LIVING PEOPLE

TRANSLATED BY SHELDON GILMAN
AND ROBERT LEVINE

NOVEMBER EDITIONS
MMXVI

Design and layout: The Curved House

ISBN 978-94-92027-07-8

NOVEMBER EDITIONS
338-II Jacob van Lennepkade
Amsterdam, 1053 NJ
The Netherlands

For inquiries please drop us a line at hello@novembereditions.com

www.NovemberEditions.com

CONTENTS

MY HEART: AN INTRODUCTION

Jakob Hessing, Professor of German Literature

The Franz Rosenzweig Research Center for German-Jewish Literature and Cultural History, The Hebrew University of Jerusalem

I

The life of Else Lasker-Schüler (1869-1945) spans the most decisive period in modern German history. She was born when Bismarck was about to create the first German nation state, she died shortly before Germany collapsed in the Second World War. It was a catastrophic ending not only for the Germans, but even more so for the Jews under Hitler. With the rise of National Socialism the poetess was forced to flee into exile, and she died far away from her native country.

The end was a disaster, but during Else Lasker-Schüler's lifetime German culture cannot be imagined without the Jews. This is especially true in the field of literature, and one finds famous German-Jewish authors and poets everywhere – in Berlin as well as in Vienna and other central European cities under Austrian influence. At the turn of the century, when Else Lasker-Schüler began to write, Arthur Schnitzler was already well known, and others like Stefan Zweig and Jakob Wassermann started upon their career; in 1912, when she published her novel *Mein Herz*, Franz Kafka was beginning to find his unique style; in 1931, while she was still in Berlin, Elias Canetti had already completed *Die Blendung*, the novel for which he would later receive the Nobel prize; and in 1945, the year of her death, Paul Celan created the first version of his Holocaust poem 'Death Fugue'.

Almost all of the German-Jewish writers were men, and perhaps this was part of the patriarchal tradition of Judaism. The number of writing women was small – Gertrud Kolmar and Rose Ausländer, or Nelly Sachs, another Nobel prize winner – and the best known among them was Else Lasker-Schüler. Her fame rests not only on the quality of her poetry, but on other reasons as well, and they will become more evident as we shall take a look at the novel which is now presented in English translation.

* * *

Else Lasker-Schüler was born in the industrial town of Wuppertal-Elberfeld. The Jews in this western part of Germany had already given up most of their heritage, and they were well integrated into society. But the newly founded Bismarck *Reich* was in search of its national identity. Many Germans did not want the Jews to have their share in it, and decades later the poetess would remember the symptoms of anti-Semitism which she was exposed to during her years in school.

In 1894 she married the physician Berthold Lasker.[1] She moved to Berlin, where she lived until Hitler came to power, and her marriage became the turning point in her life. Lasker had been raised in a religious home, but he did not adhere to the old values anymore. He had replaced them by a thorough modern education and was striving to join the *Bildungsbürgertum*, the educated German middle class.

This had been the social goal of assimilating Jews throughout the 19th century. Lasker offered his wife the affluent home of a successful doctor, but at the turn of the century a new generation of German Jews was already suspicious of bourgeois culture. In Vienna, Sigmund Freud was working on the concepts of psychoanalysis, a fundamental critique of its repressions, and in Berlin a group of iconoclastic writers was coming of age who, on the eve of the First World War, would come to be known as the Expressionists.

Else Lasker-Schüler, ten to fifteen years older than they, is their most notable forerunner. At the beginning of the new century she had already left her husband, given birth to a son whose father, most probably, was not Berthold Lasker, and she was living on the fringes of society. A sense of discontent was spreading in intellectual and artistic circles, bringing together various groups who were trying to create collective forms of a utopian counter-culture.

Lasker-Schüler joined a number of them. The one most important to her, the *Vereinigung Neue Gesmeinschaft*, had chosen Peter Hille as its prophet, a German poet who refused to live within the walls of a house and preferred to roam about the open spaces in the vicinity of Berlin. She became his disciple, and he called her 'the black swan of Israel', a famous phrase that henceforth would be a part of her growing reputation. When he died in 1904 she wrote *Das Peter*

Hille-Buch, in which the character Tino describes his wanderings with the semi-divine poet Saint Peter.

Such pious adoration betrays a religious need that does not confine itself to traditional Judaism. Lasker-Schüler's best-known collection of poems, the *Hebräische Balladen*, was written between 1902 and 1920. They recreate a number of biblical figures,[2] but they have little in common with rabbinical exegesis and serve no homiletic purpose. Her heroes are not obedient, but rebellious and bellicose. She calls them 'wild Jews' and invents them as her antithesis to a weak and disoriented German-Jewish bourgeoisie which had given in to a foreign culture.

A metaphysical desperation underlies her contempt of German Jewry. She feels that her contemporaries have lost their ties with God, and her most famous poem is a powerful lamentation. It is called 'My People':

> The rock decays
> From which I spring
> To sing my songs of God ...
> Headlong I rush from the way
> And murmur deep within,
> Seaward, distant, and alone
> Over the wailingstones.
>
> I have flowed so far away
> From the must, the ferment,
> Of my blood.
> And still, still the echo
> In me,
> When to the East, awesomely,

The decaying rock of bone,
My people,
Cries out to God.[3]

Rushing 'from the way' she is trying to isolate herself, but Else Lasker-Schüler does not succeed. The connection is too deep and too organic, it cannot be severed. The 'decaying rock' from which she intends to escape turns out to be her own petrified bone, and whatever happens to the Jews crying out for God happens to the poetess as well.

Yet the poem does not depict a narrow tribal bond. Some of its symbols are obviously Jewish: The 'wailings' refer to the Temple in Jerusalem and the millennia of exile which followed its destruction; the 'rock of bone' hints at the biblical prophecy in which the dry bones representing the people of Israel are promised a new life.[4] The rock, however, is a Jewish and a Christian symbol alike; its decay concerns both the Jews and the Germans, in whose language the poem is written. And Else Lasker-Schüler's equation of blood and wine is Christian, too. She says of her blood that it has fermented, that it has gone sour: Her desperation is Jewish and universal at the same time.

* * *

In 1903, Else Lasker-Schüler married again. Her second husband is Herwarth Walden, a Jewish writer and musician who was nine years younger than she. Walden represents a new kind of artist who is not merely weary of bourgeois culture, but totally opposed to it. In 1910 he began to publish the periodical *Der Sturm* [The Tempest], which would become a central organ of the Expressionist movement.

In the years before the outbreak of the war, Lasker-Schüler was closely associated with the efforts of this group. She had replaced the utopian circle around Peter Hille with an artistic ideology that was ready to fight for its anti-bourgeois positions, but the endeavor soon turned out to be an illusion. The war put an end to most of it, and many of its young protagonists did not return from the battlefields. Lasker-Schüler lost some of her dearest friends – among them the painter Franz Marc and the poet Georg Trakl –, and after the war she found herself more and more isolated.

Around 1912, her second marriage was already breaking down. Then, in 1927, she lost the last person to whom she had clung with all her heart: her only son, Paul, died of tuberculosis at the age of twenty-eight; and in 1933, when she was finally forced into exile, Else Lasker-Schüler was a very lonely woman.

II

The decade before 1914 was Lasker-Schüler's most creative period. With the death of Peter Hille she emancipated herself from his tutelage, and went on to establish her own poetic identity in a series of publications.[5] But the writers and artists around her were young people, and Else Lasker-Schüler was getting older. It was now that she began to change her date of birth, and for a long time it was believed that she was born in 1876.

She may have done this for personal reasons, and perhaps she wanted her marriage to Herwarth Walden to appear more natural. But there were deeper reasons for her pretense as well.

Walden was very active in the modern art scene in Berlin – he created a forum for abstract painters who were not accepted in conventional galleries, and he published their works in *Der Sturm* –, and by marrying him Else Lasker-Schüler found herself involved in the agenda of a new generation. But in the end her pretense did not work, either in the public or in the private realm. The Expressionist movement was of a universal nature, it did not concern itself with Germans or Jews, but with mankind as a whole. Soon it was pushed aside in the First World War and the ideological havoc it created.

Even before that, Else Lasker-Schüler's marriage with Herwarth Walden had broken apart. After meeting a younger woman he left the house, and it turned out to be a final separation for her. Henceforth she would live in cheap hotel rooms and never again have a place of her own.

* * *

The epistolary novel *My Heart*, written in the final stages of her marriage to Walden, was originally published in *Der Sturm* under the title *Briefe nach Norwegen* [Letters to Norway]. It appeared in the journal in 20 installments, from September 1911 to February 1912. A playful tone is established from the very beginning, but it hides a feeling of loneliness: 'Dear boys! That little Kurt has taken you with him to Sweden, Herwarth, is certainly the act of a friend. Little Kurt will become chief public prosecutor and nothing can happen to you. But something can happen to me, I have no one to whom I can tell my adventure […]' (p. 3)

Kurt Neimann was a wealthy young man, a friend, and also the lawyer, of Walden, whom he had invited for a short journey to Scandinavia in the summer of 1911. They were back in Berlin early in September, but Else Lasker-Schüler kept writing her fictitious letters to them as though they were still abroad. Nothing can happen to Walden, she says, because little Kurt will be his legal protector; but she is an outlaw without any protection. The poetess is in a constant struggle against conventional society, and she goes on to tell them of an erotic adventure which she has had the other night:

> I have never been as much in love as I am this time. If it is of interest to you: the day before yesterday I went to the Luna Park […] quietly slipping into the Egyptian exhibition […] I danced with Minn, the son of the Sultan of Morocco. We danced, danced like two dancing snakes, up on the Islamic stage, shedding our skins to the enticing tones of the bamboo flute of the snake charmer, lured on by the drums of the ancient Pharaohs, with the eternal bells […] he and I suddenly found ourselves on the way to Tangiers, shouted war-like cries, until his mouth kissed mine so gently, with such ardor, that I would have felt awkward resisting. (pp. 3–4)

Oriental phantasies are a familiar element in her poetry. They occur in the *Hebräische Balladen* as well as in her prose texts of this period, and here she uses them to signal her marital infidelity, putting it on record in *Der Sturm*, where both spouses are well-known figures.

Else Lasker-Schüler turned the crisis of her marriage to Walden into a public event. It is part and parcel of her anti-bourgeois strategy: Art had brought the two together as partners in their struggle against a philistine society, and in a work of art she notified the audience of their separation. This becomes even more obvious as she speaks of a second lover she claims to have found and describes him like a painting:

> I have fallen permanently in love with the Slav – why – only the stars know. I love him in an entirely different way from the Muslim, whose kiss still sits, a golden butterfly, on my cheek. But I would like to look at the Slav as though I were looking at a painting based on an old master. His face has the color of fire, I burn when I look at it and am drawn inexorably to it. You need not worry, Herwarth, he has not replied at all to my love letter. I wrote to him: 'Sweet Slav, had you been on display in the Louvre in Paris, I would have stolen you instead of the Mona Lisa. I would like to look at you forever; I would never grow weary of doing that […] I think of nothing else but you and only you and nothing else, as though you were standing in a frame. So beautiful as you were yesterday, you were so beautiful […] you hardly know how to deal with your own affairs, you always hang yourself in bad light.' (pp. 5–6)

Her love affairs, of course, were largely inventions, a poetic sanctuary in a world of growing loneliness. Art was her last line of defense: In a later section of the novel she writes of a portrait which a modern painter has made of her. The painter in question is Karl Schmidt-Rottluff, one of the co-founders of *Die Brücke* [The Bridge], a union of Expressionists who had found a sponsor in Herwarth Walden and the circle of people centered around the *Sturm*. Her description of the portrait makes it abundantly clear why this kind of art was hardly acceptable in pre-war Germany:

Schmidt-Rottluff painted me sitting in a tent. A man-drill who composes battle-songs, Schmidt-Rottluff has painted me as a mandrill, and I descend from the pine-apple. You have conquered the ape; but one can in no way escape one's birth.

Am enchanted with my colorful personality, my ancient fearfulness, my dangerousness, but my golden forehead, my golden eyelids, which watch over my blue composing. My mouth is as red as berries in a thicket, in my cheeks the sky ornaments itself in a blue dance, but my nose quivers towards the east, a battle-flag, and my chin is a spear, a poisoned spear. Thus I sing my solemn song. O, Herwarth, you cannot understand how it feels at all – what remains of the ape in you? Herwarth, you need not repeat this, Herwarth, I swear to you by the prophet Darwin, I am my only immortal love. (p. 74)

The Expressionist portrait of Else Lasker-Schüler brings out the ape in man, tearing down the facade of a mendacious culture. There are Jewish elements in her self-description – her nose 'quivers towards the east', and her 'solemn song', once again, refers to the *Song of Songs*, the Biblical love story –, but she goes beyond her Jewish ancestry. She reaches down into the depth of Darwinian pre-history and bares the roots of a repressive society which soon will destroy itself in the war.

The portrait described here is an actual painting, prepared by a well-known artist. In the last resort, however, the images of herself which Else Lasker-Schüler evokes in her poetry are ultimate expressions of what, to her and to many other poets of her time, art is all about – they are symbols of a precarious existence on the borderline of life and death. 'I live life like a picture, in which I am always present,' she writes in another letter:

> Sometimes the picture is hung to my disadvantage, or something moves in my setting, or I am not pleased with the frame. Frames are restrictions, non-art, borders, which no god, but a dilettante-God lays out. Round frames still have something circular, but the four-cornered ones, which are now the fashion, have, in such a completely human way, stepped out of the universe. Thus I look out of the picture at life; which of them do I take more seriously? Both. In life I perish, and in the picture breathe again. (pp. 65–6)

Art, it turns out, is a strategy of survival for Else Lasker-Schüler. She has gone through a series of crises in recent years, but now she is facing the most difficult of all. Her alliance with Walden was more than a marriage, it was a public statement in times of upheaval, and its collapse is a sort of surrender. Towards the end of the novel she upholds her defiant position one last time, but she does so with a broken heart:

> I flee into the thicket, Herwarth, I have always hated the house, even the palace itself; just call a room property and you are already domesticated. I hate domesticity, therefore hate the last confinement, the tomb. I move into the deepest forest, Herwarth […] I lie down under big trees and stretch myself out along their roots, entwined with each other like gnarled snakes. […] every beat of my heart was a dance. I can no longer dance, Herwarth; I cry – snow falls on my weeping eyes. (pp. 95–6)

III

My Heart is a series of open letters, written by a woman to her husband in the final stages of their marriage. The public sphere in which Else Lasker-Schüler situates her correspondence is the café, and there is a feeling of ambivalence about the place. One is not too happy there, but no one can do without it. 'Secretly we all think of the café as the devil,' she writes, 'but what would life be without the devil?'

The bohemians meet in the Café des Westens on Berlin's main boulevard, the Kurfürstendamm.[6] The artists call it 'Café Größenwahn' [Café Megalomania], and a touch of irony pervades Else Lasker-Schüler's novel as well. It tells a double-edged story. On the one hand it creates a world of its own, an artistic counter-culture within Berlin's society; but on the other hand it constantly gives away the futility of this counter-culture, the fact that these artists can do nothing to change a threatening reality which will soon lead to self-destruction.

The decline of Else Lasker-Schüler's second marriage is a metaphor for this situation. When Herwarth Walden leaves her for a younger woman, she loses contact with a whole generation, and this is more than a personal tragedy. In art and literature, the agenda of the Expressionist movement was swept away by the First World War, and in the Weimar Republic the counter-culture of the Café Größenwahn no longer existed. German society was torn apart by a brutal struggle for political supremacy, and the victory of the Nazis spelled the end for any modernism in Germany. Hitler himself was an artist of sorts before he turned to politics, and after his rise to power everything reminiscent of Expressionism was forced into oblivion.

By then, Else Lasker-Schüler had already left Germany. She will live in exile for another twelve years, at first in Switzerland, and during the Second World War in Jerusalem. She will go on to write a number of important works, among them her anti-fascist play *IchundIch* [I-and-I] and her last collection of poems *Mein blaues Klavier* [My Blue Piano], but nowhere will she be able to reconstruct the sense of common cause pervading the letters of *My Heart*. It had been an illusion even then, and her novel describes its approaching end. But it gave her strength in the most productive years of her creative life.

NOTES

1. Berthold Lasker was the brother of Emanuel Lasker, the famous chess player who was world champion from 1894 to 1921.

2. Among them there are Cain and Abel, Abraham and Isaac, Hagar and Ismael, Jacob and Esau, Joseph and the Pharaoh, Moses and Josua, Saul and David, Boas, Ruth and Sulamith.

3. "My People", in: Else Lasker-Schüler, *Hebrew Ballads and Other Poems.* Translated, edited, and with an introduction by Audri Durchslag and Jeanette Litman-Demeestère, The Jewish Publication Society of America, Philadelphia 1980.

4. Cf. Ezekiel 37, 4-5: 'Again he said to me, Prophesy over these bones, and say to them, O dry bones, hear the word of the Lord. Thus says the Lord God to these bones; Behold, I will cause breath to enter into you, and you shall live.'

5. She published several volumes of poetry, *Der siebente Tag* (1905), *Meine Wunder* (1911), and an early version of *Hebräische Balladen* (1912); wrote the play *Die Wupper* (1909), and created an artistic persona for herself in prose works like *Die Nächte Tino von Bagdads* (1907), *Gesichte* (1913), and *Der Prinz von Theben* (1914).

6. For a description of the scene, see Sigrid Bauschinger, *Else Lasker-Schüler. Biographie*, Wallstein Verlag, Göttingen 2004, pp. 172ff. Bauschinger's biography is a comprehensive and very informative study on the poetess and her social surroundings.

MY HEART

Dedicated to Adolf Loos

DEAR BOYS!

That little Kurt has taken you with him to Sweden, Herwarth, is certainly the act of a friend. Little Kurt will become chief public prosecutor and nothing can happen to you. But something can happen to me; I have no one to whom I can tell my adventures except Peter Baum, who, however, is moving out of his old place into a new one. In his confusion he carried his Matja instead of his writing table into the moving van, entrusting the moving men not to tear the tassels. In the evening I first told him my new love story. For I have never been as much in love as I am this time. If it is of interest to you: the day before yesterday I went to the Luna Park with Gertrude Barrison, quietly slipping into the Egyptian exhibition, as though we had a premonition of something sweet. In a coffee house Gertrude caught the attention of an Arab with a full beard; she was totally horrified at my suggestion to flirt with him. I had, you see, gazed at the curl of his lips, which had now stiffened in response to the coolness of my companion. Her reluctance bothered me very much. But during the belly dancing one of the miracles of my Arabian book happened; I danced with Minn, the son of the sultan of Morocco. We danced, danced like two dancing snakes, up on the Islamic stage, shedding our skins to the enticing tones of the bamboo flute of the snake charmer, lured on by the drum of the ancient Pharaohs, with the eternal bells. And Gertrude also danced the craquette, but like a muse, not as Muslim-like as we; she danced with graceful, provocative arms, her fingers waving like fringes. But he and I suddenly found ourselves on the way to Tangiers, shouted war-like cries, until his mouth kissed me so gently, with such ardor, that I would have felt awkward resisting. Ever since I have loved everyone whose skin color has a trace of his skin color, reminding me of his gold brocade. I love the Slav, because he has brown hair like Minn; I love the bishop, because the ruby in his tie is made of the red dye with which my royal Muslim paints his nails. I cannot, without burning, think of his eyes; narrow, meandering rivers, shimmering irises, whose bed is the Nile. What should I do? The management of the Luna Park, apparently having become suspicious, has forbidden me to enter the park. You see, yesterday morning I brought my wonderful friend a large diamond – yours, Herwarth; are you angry? – together with a bag of cocoanut candies. Suppose I really had some money now! And I have written a firm letter to the Luna Park, that I would report the insult inflicted upon me to Voss, that my name is Else Lasker-Schüler, and I had supplied occasional verse for the Khediv at the reception of European crown princes. What good is it that they let me in now – a detective is always following me, but Minn and I meet at the Zulus, who live, black and wild, in the seamy area of the Egyptian exhibition, which no white man ever sees. I got into this mess because of the impresario, who treats the Muslim people like slaves, and I shall kill him with my dagger, which I bought in Minn's land. He is the youngest that the slave-trader brought to Europe, he is son of the son of the son of the most youthful looking father in the Egyptian Luna garden. He is no slave, Minn is a king's son, Minn is a warrior, Minn is my biblical playmate. He wears an arrogant satin gown and he dreams only of me, because he has kissed me. Little Kurt, friend Herwarth, would that you were here, no one will go with me to Egypt; yesterday a marriage was announced there on all the billboards. Can it be that he got married?

Just think, I looked at the moon on the Weidendammer bridge for twenty cents. I got only a very shadowy acquaintance with the people through the telescope. One man had his hair cut like you, Herwarth, or should I say not cut off. Are the working people on the moon also always asking you to cut your hair? And I saw a gentleman with a briefcase eating bread with roast beef, who looked like you, little Kurt. And really, there is a café on the moon; it was night, from inside the café I heard a voice like Dr. Caro's singing: 'Then let us speak again of love, as once in May'.

I have fallen permanently in love with the Slav – why – only the stars know. I love him in an entirely different way from the Muslim, whose kiss still sits, a golden butterfly, on my cheek. But I would like to look at the Slav as though I were looking at a painting based on an old master. His face has the color of fire, I burn when I look at it and am drawn inexorably to it. You need not worry, Herwarth, he has not replied at all to my love letter. I wrote to him: 'Sweet Slav, had you been on display in the Louvre in Paris, I would have stolen you instead of the Mona Lisa. I would like to look at you forever;

I would never grow weary of doing that, I would have them build me a tower, without doors. I would most like to come to you when you are asleep, so that your eyelash did not blink in the frame. I think of nothing else but you and only you and nothing else, as though you were standing in a frame. So beautiful as you were yesterday, you were so beautiful, one feels drawn to steal you twice, once from the world and once from yourself; you hardly know how to deal with your own affairs, you always hang yourself in bad light.' I assure you again, Herwarth, you need not concern yourself about this, yesterday evening he never once offered me his hand. Someone told me in confidence, he doesn't want to be at odds with you, he is a writer. What do you say to such cowardice? In his place you would have written back to me, wouldn't you? You don't need to come any longer; two nights ago I even dreamt that a polar bear met the two of you north-pole travelers and asked you whether you would permit yourselves to be photographed with him.

What exceptional unhappiness I have in love! You too? Have you already seen Ibsen and Hedda Gabler? And have you looked at another landscape yet, like a café? Up there, there are probably only fields of snow and white mountains and who knows what else? The Laps won't do, but send me a couple of Greenlanders.

Laugh if you want, but I haven't slept the whole night; first it's cold, then it's hot, then fall storms in, and in the interval your midnight sun glows. As though September was mimicking me! I certainly don't know exactly whom I love: the Slav or the bishop? Or will I ever be able to part from Minn? Yesterday I appointed the bishop an archbishop. But the Slav will prudently submit his resignation soon, his diplomatic experiments with me are democratic. I asked him to return my love letter, damn it. I have, damn it, self-respect in my bones. He has not yet sent it back – I wonder if he will write a couple of words to me! But what help would that be now, the archbishop speaks, as I imagine, exactly so, and also understands how to fulfill my unspoken wishes. He wanders with me through melancholy woods, along paths of roses, or we sought out, during the ghost hours, cracked streets that look upon the Spree river, dark as the eye of a worker. And every day I receive a letter from the bishop, they are the loveliest letters that I had ever read; I read them aloud in the voice of the Slav. And how are things going for you? May I assume that you have reached the region of the snow hen by now? Don't catch a cold, Herwarth. Above all don't get the sniffles, a running nose is driving me crazy. Are you coming home soon? The archbishop and the Slav got up today before eleven o'clock and left the café. I would gladly have gone off with them unceremoniously, really, but you still don't know the people in the café. Suppose the archbishop and the Slav are telling each other everything!!? The fat Caius-Maius didn't budge from my table; if only he didn't always talk about literature! As long as it is about my verses it is bearable, but when he begins to chatter about Aristophanes, he should be dragged off to Dante's hell! He confided to me that he loves Lucretia Borzia. When I asked him who the lady might be, he laughed convulsively. Without you, Herwarth, things here are not working out: you always help me with the story, and then I'm embarrassed to ask anyone to help me dot my i's. Yesterday your friend, the doctor, suddenly appeared in the café with Marie Borchardt and her friend, Margret König. She is an actress, did you know that? You know, she is charming! I sent her, in empty packets of cigarettes smoked by the Slav, chocolate cookies and a cigarette. She is a sweet silhouette. I always see her standing before me, a golden nymph, among my splashing, gaily colored thoughts. That's why I went this evening to Marie Borchardt's talk, not to hear my poems, but because of Margret. But I was very surprised by Marie's reading (she speaks Italian); her voice resonates with the sounds of Venetian glass flowers, and genuine lace from the palazzi crackles among her words. In her terra cotta dress and her turban with gold fringes, she looked like a little Doge's princess. Had I known a Doge, I would have had her carried off in a gondola. But am I the only one to whom the same things happen every day? You always say that I should not bother with other people, but if the artistic in life provides me pleasure, so too the inartistic is a source of annoyance. I believe it is now twelve o'clock; I am really too frightened today to step into the hallway of my apartment alone. I am edgy. I shall not be able to keep my word to you to be in bed before morning. I shall go sleep at the ticket agent's place in the Halenseer railroad station, on her bloodless, old sofa. She tells me, during the remainder of the night, about her lovers. Goodnight, Herwarth, dear little Kurt!

For two evenings now I have not been in the café, my heart has been bothering me. Doctor Döblin from Urban came with his dear girlfriend to offer a diagnosis. He thinks that I am suffering from a thyroid condition, but actually I have a longing for the café. He insisted, however, on getting rid of my thyroid, which is pressing indirectly on my heart; he says that it might make me a little cretinous, but since I am so sharp-witted, I would soon be my old self. I have, you see, confessed that I had wanted to use the gas pipe to end my life because of my two friends; the whole gas pipe has been taken out. I could not pay the gas bill. I could not even drown myself in milk, since Bolle does not bring it anymore. How shall I come back to the café now without blushing? A person like me must keep her word. I shall make up some story, so that the bishop and the Slav will think that you will be too frightened.

DEAR BOYS

Just think, neither of them was there when I, still alive, arrived at the café around noon, but your friend the doctor sat singing to himself, sometimes so loud he nearly forgot where he was. His voice is mythic, Olympian, and like a smoking crater, and it can thunder like the word of Zeus. How utterly inartistic to be angry with one another.

Guess who rang me up early this morning – Fridolin Guhlke. He says that he is in love, that he has found his first love; that it happened three years ago, when she was just thirteen. And he is on the wagon now; his flame seems to wear a halo around her head. Also, he says that he never comes to the café anymore, and I should promise him to be as ascetic as he. Secretly we all think of the café as the devil, but what would life be without the devil? I am curious how long Guhlke can hold out without the devil. Sometimes things get overwrought here, when an overdressed plebeian sneers at you one should get out of her way; it's hard for her to get by with her big bust covered by a lace stole. I wanted to box her ears when she went upstairs to the billiard room to get her husband, who approached me, accompanied by Galician Sadducees and Chaldeans. But I kept quiet; I hate getting involved with loud, screaming women. After a while two policemen arrived, to question me. But Richard hid me between two newspapers; that is now my pigeon-hole. Then our Director Wauer arrived, he would have enjoyed watching that scene. I made that up to him, however. He didn't really know the actors in the Egyptian Luna Park. Just at that moment the dromedary trotted by the window of the café; it came from the zoo, it had problems with its stomachs. I longed for Minn, he wasn't the one who had gotten married. Which reminds me, little Kurt, Herwarth forgot his handkerchiefs, lend him one of yours. You'll get it back washed. It is four o'clock, it is still daylight. Director Wauer leads our little caravan in his car.

Dear Herwarth and dear little Kurt! Stay as long as you like; I am so pleased that you have recovered, and that you have sent such beautiful, interesting picture postcards. How well is Ibsen's tomb kept, a pillar in the language of hieroglyphics, a northern pyramid. Yesterday the archbishop also showed me my monument. It would be nice if the Indian tower in the Luna Park someday stood over my body. Fear overcame me, but at the same time, ennobled, I bent my head in recognition of the honor accorded me. The bishop is the gardener of the word, he speaks with an even calmness that is comforting. He even maintains that he speaks so evenly and carefully only with me, and I don't know whether he takes me for a delicate kind of plant or a tiger. In the evening, when we met the Slav, he walked right by us; in an old-fashioned way he plays the sublime one, he is elderly even in youth. If someone is elderly, he can experience no season of the heart, not even winter, just as someone who is childish knows nothing of spring. O, the change in people means everything; the bishop and I are playing spring at the moment. Peter Baum agrees entirely with me that he is too lazy to change. He sends you greetings; his novel about the Rococo period is ready, for nearly half a year it has been ready. Farewell, dear comrades!

Caius-Maius, the Emperor, sat mysteriously at my table when Peter Baum went off for a moment; Caius wanted to ask me something. 'I want to ask you something, Else Lasker-Schüler, pay attention! It's about my literary, as well as my material future. Would Mr. Walden take it badly if I went with the publisher Capuletti in Florence? Kraus is above all that, but on one such occasion in the past Walden had offered Mr. D. the alternative.' I answered him, Herwarth, that he overestimated my standing with you. I was not even a go-for in the office, but was applying for the position of secretary, and would bring up his concern. Now, am I so dumb? Admittedly I am really very fond of Caius-Maius, he is a droll, adult, chubby-cheeked angel, a Dionysus turned pious, in a Dionysian suit; he has preserved his sense of humor, but instead of a bunch of grapes he wears a white tie around his neck. How people change, what literature makes of people! But, in all seriousness, Herwarth, will you hold it against him? I'll tell you only once, if you publish no more of his work, I won't write another word. The only things that give me pleasure are Caius-Maius things. When Peter Baum came back to our table, the ladies Marie and Margret came through the door of the café. I said that today Margret looked like a little glow-worm, and Peter Baum reached for her. But Caius-Maius went on swimming through the literary bliss like a whale. From his head a fountain flowed over his back. We went home early, Herwarth, on my honor! Another letter has come from the Dalai Lama in Vienna, I have stuck it into the other letters and cards and printed matter in your five-o'clock trousers.

DEAR COOK AND PEARY!

I must entrust you with a secret: yesterday evening, the sky was a mixture of dull gray and stars, the bishop and I went into a little bar in Mommenstrasse. But I had no more money with me than would pay for a glass of water. The bishop, however, could drink huge amounts of alcohol; he only wanted to drink Burgundy, white Burgundy. He declared that white Burgundy flowed through his heart, he wanted to let me know of his pure love through the fragrance of wine. But I told him that I had no money. And he was crest-fallen that I would take nothing from him. Do you think that I should have drunk Burgundy with him? Or Danziger? I'll tell you straight out, we drank Danziger; I let a person pay for me for the first time; there was a delicacy in his giving, at times he lifted the small, finely cut glass to my lips the way one does it for a child. Since that moment I have loved the bishop, and I have permitted him to kiss my hair; he says that it smells of lavender.

DEAR BOYS!

There's not a soul here to whom I can tell these things, come back soon! Peter Baum is a sheep, he is always grazing on the meadow at his mother's house, and he can never get away from Hans or some other cousin from Wuppertal. Either his sister clings to him, or his wife Maja has returned from a trip. Without Peter Baum I cannot live. He never reproaches me, he finds that everything I do is an expression of who I am. But I am afraid of you, dear Herwarth; I would prefer being slapped rather than looking at your severe face. This is how I used to feel at school. And I would rather, in your absence, send these letters to you and little Kurt in your publishing house. Yet you say that it's not right, but everything is possible, if there is good will. Peter Baum sees no harm in it. I waited for him all day yesterday; three times I sent the same letter to him, one to his first house, the second to his second house, and the last to his mother's place in Friedenau. In Wuppertal Plattdeutsch: 'Dear Peter Baum, the last time that I write to you: come or don't come, old man. I have so much to tell you, I don't know which of three workers I love: Frederick or Wilhelm, or the East Prussian. You must help me remember, I'm such a dummy. Why were you put on earth? Lend me some pennies, I have no more potatoes in the house, or anything to eat. I'll pay you back when my tragedy of occasion, *Die Wupper*, is produced. Director Reinhardt has promised to put it on, if only the old grandfather in the first act doesn't die first; he suffers from the weather, as you know. And Grätz of the German theater will play him. That should rile you up, old clown? Are you coming or what? Come on! Your Amanda.'

Just think, he has gone off with his sister Julie to Hiddensee. At Hohenzollerndamm his wife, Matja, is living with her friend Jenni. Peter Baum has left his novel lying in old

Ringbahnstrasse. The paperhangers have smeared half the pages with paste, to glue them under the new wallpaper. But what does that have to do with us! Did you get your letter from the post office in Christiana, dear Herwarth? What do you have to say about the popularity of your pantomime throughout Luxemburg? I'm still singing: 'I am the count of Luxemburg and have squandered, have squandered my wealth.'

DEAR CHILDREN!

I have something frightfully painful to tell you right away: the Moroccan has been kidnapped by a woman who is certainly not a lady.

HERWARTH!

Yesterday a monster with orange-blond curls pasted on her head was in the café and seemed to be waiting for you all morning, Herwarth. Don't tell me that you know her; she talks in your accent, with all of your ways of expressing yourself. Then she went into the telephone-booth; I, together with witnesses, heard her say your name, but your secretary had probably already left, since the monster stomped her feet so angrily that the glass door of the booth rattled. Only intimates stomp like that! It would be low of you to be untrue to me. Someone in the café saw how she slipped under the table for you one of her artificial, orange-colored locks. But what was the other thing I wanted to mention: this morning Minn was at my place; on his proud shoulders he carried a huge suitcase in which to pack me off to Tangiers. I must give some more thought to the bishop; certainly if he really loves me, I can't just leave. But one more thing: no one was more enchanted with your pantomime than the archbishop and the Slav. So take your time at the North Pole, you and little Kurt.

DEAR HERWARTH!
TO YOUR HEALTH, LITTLE KURT!

Yesterday my Rosa and I were almost mugged. She was just patching up my skirt. It was her guy, who had seemed so harmless. Recently she wrote to him the same letters to you and little Kurt that I had read aloud to her. All the things that we have to go through! Financially I am having problems. I am deep in debt at the café, with the afternoon waiter: pheasant with rice and apple sauce; with the midnight waiter: veal cutlet with broiled potatoes and cranberries and a vanilla ice, a total of fifty cents. Martha Hellmuth, the sorceress Hellmuthe in my Saint-Peter-Hille book, lent me ten cents for the trip home, otherwise I could not have kept my word to you again. And then along came attorney Caro; he certainly is a gentleman, he gave me ten marks, indicating that he owes you that. When I had eaten salmon with butter sauce I thought of it as an elegant apology from him. Having no money certainly is disastrous. Having only a little money is even worse, I am not accustomed to living on a small scale. Don't worry about me, as long as I have something to pawn when I am in dire circumstances – your Croesus.

DEAR BOYS!

Höxter suspects that I am enchanted with Minn, he brought me two picture postcards of the Egyptian exhibit at the Luna Park, which show my Sultan seated on the camel in a palm-tree landscape. To what land has that thieving woman carried him off? By the way, Herwarth, have you had a negative plate made of the drawing which Höxter made of me? Is it going to appear in *Der Sturm*? I look like the warrior Prince of Thebes, for whom, by contrast, the Sphinx in the foreground is a real woman. (Otherwise I shall not write another word for *Der Sturm*). Höxter and I sit today all alone in the front garden of the café, in the sun, imagining that we both are descended from Bedouins; he and I are sitting on noble Arabian steeds, and this is our protection. We are of the race of kings, and in our thoughts battle other tribes. I am grateful to Höxter, he told me a fantasy, his sister's name is Schlomé.

Do you know who was with me yesterday? The ex-queen Eugenie! I timidly opened the door of the hall, frightened that it was the bailiff. Her majesty promised to write to my cousin, who is her twin millionairess.

DEAR HERWARTH, NOBLE LITTLE KURT!

A few days ago I decided that Karl Kraus, the Dalai Lama in Vienna, should also become the minister. The only way I can picture him is sitting on an impressive chair. If people were not so boring and tedious, he would have been made minister long ago. Do you think I might become court-poet, with all rights and privileges? But that's less important to me. I would have brought up the matter of the Dalai-Lama long before, but people always smile wearily at what I say, and if I say something, they do not understand how to use the tight-rope to catch my playful words. Only the minister enjoys my leaps, he is serious enough.

Little Jakobsohn has subscribed to twenty-two numbers of *Die Fackel*; I told you right away, Herwarth, he is not so bad, *Der Sturm* will be his undoing. Have a good time, both of you, don't worry about my dowry, I have diamonds and pearls – and a pile of verse – composed about you.

I can only write you a postcard today; the bishop just phoned, suggesting that we take a bit of a walk in Siberia. We call the area around Lutzowerplatz in Charlottenburg Siberia. In any event, we have many similar perceptions about the world. We also see the same animals in people's faces. He loves cats, I don't. I'll ask him today if he loves cats more than me. Such questions give him pleasure. I ask him many frightful things in French, as though he were my superior. It is so refreshing when suddenly all the burdensome thoughts and imbedded feelings glide from one's shoulders and one becomes a marionette, pulled about in fine silk strings. But sometimes I am his golden ball, which he lovingly tosses into the hands of children. Or I fall asleep, drunk with his words, he has something of the quality of grapes. Since I met him I often lean on the black painted walls of houses and become sweet. If only he did not consider me a plaything! I might wither away in the emptiness of Berlin. Even the earth here is buried under asphalt; now they want to construct a canopy, like the Wintergarten's dreary starry heaven, over the capital; where then can anyone see blue? For me, the western part of our city is the most hateful, the working-class areas at least have something war-like about them. Recently we were standing at night on the bridge which leads to the Siemens factory. We would almost have kissed, but I avoided his lips, instinctively; we are also both too white, if we were to blush while kissing, it would be like blood, perhaps like murder. I must tell you all these things, love me for it.

DEAR BOYS!

When I entered the café today, the Slav and the bishop sat off by themselves. The Slav seems to find it apparently more politic in your absence, Herwarth, to have nothing to do with me, he plays the nobleman. The idea hasn't dawned on me yet that I mean nothing to him, but I am tired of him; in addition, he is not as good-looking as when I first saw him, he has a cramped expression on his face. And he is always pleased if someone loses his imagination, since he has none. I have lost Minn; all the Moroccan dreams and the tattooed half moon on his quivering nostril. Across the room the bishop saw me crying, he sympathetically kissed the head of his sacred cat at least 23 times.

Today I presented to the bishop a singer, because she resembles the talismanic photograph which he carries in his wallet. Now let him really see his type face-to-face. I certainly believe that he is only trying to get my goat, but revenge is going to be fun. Felicitas is always humming my melodies, which I know from the East, in Berlin jargon; she is my watered-down Nile, alternating with my bowl of water from the Tigris, in which she washes her stockings. But she wears silk stockings; the bishop noticed that with pleasure, he also made comparisons between me and her. I don't like that about him, I think I don't like him anymore. My whole psyche has been split for some time now. My soul is a fine city made entirely of gold, with nothing but covered paths leading from one palace to another. And its landscapes surpass the beauties of all other countries. Am I sick again, but where? They have run out of mosaic tile there, and they render me in brick. When I left I offered my hand to the bishop with a smile: 'Farewell, archbishop, you claim to love Egyptian culture above all, and forget that one must not juxtapose a Pharaonic princess (even in the mind) with a German porcelain goose.' That's what I said to him.

HERWARTH!

Today we had cold cuts again; and what I really like to eat is duck and yellow plums. I simply longed for Kempinski's, in spite of the greedy Philistines at the next table. Why are we both still so unmarried? In the café I am neither your admirer nor your companion, nor your betrothed. There you are my lover, first lover, and I certainly felt that in the two times we ate there the talent to be a bon vivant lay hidden in you as it lies hidden in all men; but I have existed not only as the poetess and Tino of Baghdad, not only as the Prince of Thebes, as well as Jussuf the Egyptian, but I can also be a very little girl, who has been invited for the first time to dinner at Kempinski's by a gentleman, and discovers a taste for caviar and duck with plum sauce, but who still shudders with fear at the sight of snails on the half-shell. Do you still recall how we were afraid that someone we knew would see us – our relationship. I drank red wine from your glass, and you complimented me on my slender ankles. You promised to buy me silk stockings and a white feather for my big straw hat. You spoke with such honeyed sweetness to me, especially when I embarrassedly chose something in addition from the selection of jams. And I really forgot that I was your wife, and I made fun of your old lady, and her dark forehead. But I never shall forget your perplexed face; right then I knew that you had often dined at Kempinski's with little girls, who made fun of your wife's fanatical Galilean forehead. That had always been enough to distract you from your little sweethearts, because you were gruff and annoyed with me for having insulted your 'wife.' And as I have learned, you were there again recently, in a little party; your friend, the doctor, brought his smiling little girl with him. Why didn't you urge Kurt to invite the doctor also on the trip to Norway? He seemed worn out and angry. There was no one more in need of attentive love than the doctor, than 'our' doctor; he and I are in perfect harmony. For many years I have sent flowers to young men who look like him.

DEAR NORTH POLE EXPLORERS!

This morning Director Wauer received a telegram from Elberfeld. The city of Elberfeld has informed him that the Wuppertal singing group will serenade him, because he is performing my little piece. My hometown people really like me! And a deputation of dyers, button-makers, and two hundred weavers will make the presentation of an album of photographs of the mountains to the director. I am wild about director Wauer.

DEAR BOTH OF YOU!

How does Richard Weiss in Vienna know about the production of my play? He sent me roses today. I'd like to see him once more. In his writings all of his poems are printed, some are bent trees, but fine domed structures also rise on the banks. Yes, his writing has banks and rivers, sacred waves, like fragrant prayers. His writing is fragrant. Someone revealed to me that he is thin, has brown hair, and his eyes have a pained look; like me, he parts his hair on one side. When I think about him, I am always very touched: I wished that I were a clown and he a snake, I would teach him to dance.

DEAR HERWARTH AND DEAR KURT!

Ah, I had such a strange dream tonight! I lay on a bier in the middle of a square. I lay wrapped in a broad, silent cloth, as though in an ocean – and was dead. At times you came up to me, Herwarth, and lifted the sea from my face and pointed to my forehead. The number of people who have mocked me equals the number of days I have lived. I began to grow angry because of your naiveté, for I have always hated the curious, impertinent day. But when night came I implored you to bestow upon three princesses my love. You solemnly promised to send me the bracelet of the Venus of Siam, that

I wore while composing my poems. You repeated to me, with clear voice, to hand my ring, with the evening gleaming in its setting, to the gentle lawyer's wife, who is always singing about May. You swore to me faithfully that you yourself would place my ruby heart around the neck of Nora of India, the white panther, my true Absalon, my playmate. I wept so wildly, I heard the sea rising around me. And I was afraid that your finger would be caught as it grew over the place, upon which I lay, the clear sign-post which pointed to my forehead. We are always waiting for something – Zeuxis Kokoschka strolled behind the Dalai-Lama; and Loos, the gorilla-architect, carried in his hands my vaults, which is my due, made of Lebanese wood, smooth, but too rich for the vain taste of the people. And a struggle broke out around the house of my body; plaster moulds and carvings were placed on the facade of my temple. But I could no longer struggle, I had already turned aside from the diurnal, and played with undifferentiated time. The eyes of the Dalai-Lama, blue, gentle myrrh, embalmed me; Zeuxis painted me finally in death. And you, Herwarth, kissed my forehead, an organ symphony rose up within me; I am incomparable; I always could be only what others see in me, since my forehead was the night sky. You knew it.

DEAR REINDEER!

I am so looking forward to your antlers! But it occurred to me that you wouldn't easily get away from sledding. And therefore I have made short work of my letters to you. Because of this I have received many inquiries expressing regret; therefore stay there for a while, endure the cold a bit. I shall begin to collect my letters to you, and publish them later under the title, 'Heart-letters, the only true manual designed for writing love letters, legally protected.' All existing manuals of love-letters provoke nausea and stomach-ache. A manufacturer of porcelain will have to design the cover for me, a couple between picturesque floral patterns. Oesterheld and Cohn say this is my first reasonable idea, only their proof-reader Knoblauch is shocked by it. But the publisher has not yet recovered from the flop of my *Wupper*. And what do you think – the miller who mills mills has sent back my manuscript of essays from Munich, 'although they are lovely, the public is not interested in the names.' But I think that Julius Lieban, Emmy Destinn, Tilla Durieux, William Wauer, Paul Lindau, Friedrich von Schennis, Peter Baum, St. Peter Hille, Karl Kraus, Adolf Loos, Oskar Kokoschka, Dr. Adolf Kerr, Maupassant etc, are not unknown people. Moreover, all of my essays appeared in leading newspapers and magazines, that should be a yardstick for the miller who mills mills. Your bad luck.

HERWARTH AND KURT!

Tonight I must tell you something very strange. I just ran into Stefan George in the darkness. He wore a black velvet jacket, let his shoulders droop as though weary from the weight of the wing. I screamed very loudly. I had met an archangel, like the one painted in Dürer's picture.

DEAR HERWARTH AND KURT!

I am tired of the café, but that does not mean that I'm going to say farewell to it forever, or to go there in some gypsy wagon. On the contrary, I shall continue to spend time there often. All day yesterday the door opened and shut, like a bazaar; not everything is the real thing: imitation poets, false verbal embellishments, simulated thinking, cigarettes smoked as an affection. For a long time now the lawyer no longer comes in. Why is one drawn so to the café! Every evening a corpse is drawn to the upper room; it cannot rest. Why do people really stay in Berlin? In this cold, unpleasant city. Berlin is an irrefutable clock; we know that she, side-by-side with time, is always watching, always letting you know where art is on the clock. And I would like to sleep through time.

Children, I am terribly bored, all my loved ones have betrayed me. I feel like an outcast when I enter the forecourt of our café. I can no longer bear the Slav. And the bishop is too valuable to me to play with; if he could bear the game! But who can bear the leaping of the mind and heart! These women who are no ladies have been Minn's undoing; I don't know whether he is still here in Berlin. I am empty, like odorless Siberia. I am so alone; were I at least lonely, then I could make poetry out of it. I am the last shade of abandonment, nothing comes after. But if only someone would say something sweet to me! Would that I were a bee and could make honey for myself! What good do your dear letters and postcards do me? I know you and you know me, we can no longer surprise each other, and I can only live on miracles. Invent a miracle, please!

Yesterday evening I was in the Wintergarden with the painter Gangolf. I enjoy going with him to the vaudeville shows. He doesn't mock them, he can stare wide-eyed, like a child. Sometimes a romantic feeling overcomes us – then he looks furtively at the carnation or rose or dahlia with which my hand is playing. Then I push it, without any reason, into his lap. Our favorites are the two musical clowns, one of whom in the white-face mask of Kubeik, who was supposedly himself hidden behind it. The other, dressed like Rubinstein, played the way Rubinstein must have played. Yes, yes, one must be a clown to be understood by the public, and – that's the way to get someplace with them. I have said it to you many times, Herwarth, I shall play Augustus and speak through my nose about my fakir and my Ached-Bey and my poetry. Gangolf was moved by it – in the evening he showed me, as a distraction, his puppet theater. He has created a city of miniature people. In addition, his paintings were actually created from the variegated blood of colors. I was sorry that he had destroyed his excellent self-portrait, the man behind the window looking out over the towers of the city. The city lost him and he lost the city. Now we intend to go to the vaudeville show together more often. You don't have anything against that, Herwarth, do you? Best wishes!

DEAR SKIERS!

Or don't you go skiing? How can I ask such superficial questions, and yet be extremely anxious about where to place my manuscript? After all, I must feed a family, I mean my Paul with all his flattering names. Now he wants a locomotive with four or forty volts of electric power or a 50-horsepower steam engine that can handle 100 cubic meters every day. I no longer ask him to reduce his demands; he is angry about my ignorance in technical matters. I believe he is Edison, and he will wait at most only one more month for me to open a shop and sell everything a penny cheaper. Perhaps he is right, he also rejects my books, and I have copied my play from Schiller. If you could only see his model for his new airplane, he is constantly talking about propellers to me. Tomorrow I must know everything by heart. What I have given birth to!! Where now can I place my manuscript quickly? Look for a young, courageous Norwegian publisher. This afternoon Paul goes out with big Caro, both of them have the same girlfriend.

DEAR BOYS!

I visited Mrs. Franziska Schultz. Her orphanage for new-born babies is so Easter-like. Nothing but little pinkish-red sugar Easter-eggs, side-by-side, peek out, hidden on white pillows. It's so charming to see, and a black chick also lay among them – a good example of black and white art. I wish that I also were still small. Sometimes I really wish that someone would take me out for a walk and I were only four years old. Time is pressing, time is deadly. Therefore it would be good to go back into childhood frequently.

This evening I would like to say to you only: Berlin is a small city, every day it shrinks more and more. A city is big only if it offers a wide perspective. Berlin has only a peephole, a bottleneck, and generally it is corked up, even imagination suffocates. Good night!

DEAR BROTHERS!

I am beside myself, Peter Baum, whom I made famous in *Der Sturm*, writes the following picture postcard to me, word-for-word: 'Dear Tino, although I find that everything suits you, yet everything does not suit me. I must insist finally that my family be left out of this entire matter. I read the low-German letter in *Der Sturm*. Warmest greetings from Hiddensee. Peter Baum.'

Do you have the words – perhaps in some kind of North-Pole-language? I need them to calm my anger. But I know something you don't know. But I have sworn not to repeat it, in spite of how it affects me personally. Why does someone actually defend himself, one should not be suspicious of oneself. It makes me unhappy that I must keep all this to myself. If only some creature would force me to do so. Or at least Peter Baum would come here and I might shout it into nature. Aren't you curious?

DEAR COMRADES!

My oath became a compulsive idea, or, better put, I could not repress it. Damned Caius-Maius came up to me today in the Spittelmarkt, where Krögel street is, and said that I seemed to be suffering from depression. His mother, however

(Dr. Hiller has a very young, charming mother), found that I seemed very cheerful. 'That I certainly am, I am happy, and can't say why to anyone. A week ago my cousin Therese, who lives on Tiergartenstrasse, sent me 200 marks. But why shouldn't I buy a hooded coat for myself!' Mother and son promised me not to repeat it to anyone. Relieved then, I sat down on the banks of the Spree, with the rest of the 200 marks. All these practical, unnecessary items, which I have bought for my millions of people – at least I would still own the hooded coat. Don't these people owe me a lot? Krögel is a fitting place, Krögel is the most beautiful spot in Berlin; that's the way I think of the fjords in Norway, like the view of the Spree suddenly, unexpectedly lying there, then dropping off into old, narrow, rutting lanes. Only flags must be blowing over the shores of the fjords – here, during the night, the small blue and white striped ice-cream trucks, which carry frozen raspberry and woodruff juice for poor children. If you see a rose, say hello to it for me.

Why don't I tell you more about the bishop? He says that I am always speaking about myself. I believe he is fed up. And yet he discovered only a small town in me, He didn't even conquer one of my cities. He ended up a hundred thousand miles from Baghdad. But who knows about my heart? Everyone is only concerned about the map. I lie between ocean and desert, a mammoth. My structure is terrifying and impressive. Please don't be frightened. But I must really try to stop talking about myself, like Kokoschka in Vienna, who never speaks about himself. Just think, Herwarth, the poster for the New Secession was in the café. That is Pechstein's wife. She is really Indian, the wonderfully beautiful daughter of the red vulture; she is picturesquely ferocious, she wore a purple gown with yellow fringes. And many painters were in the café today: Berneis, Ali Hubert, the sky-painter, and Fritz Lederer. He is Rübezahl's son. He and his brand-new wife showed me their new place; I had to drink tea with them. Through the cracks of the door of his studio the cold is always blowing. He paints only snow-pictures. You could make snowballs from the snow which lies on the huge mountains of his Bohemian homeland. I drink tea there every evening now.

TELEGRAM.

Walden-Niemann. Norway. Hotel Sea-dog. Hiller, Kurtz, Hoddis have again reached a reconciliation. Else.

DEAR CHILDREN!

I entered the café and scarcely could believe my eyes, everyone was seated together, reconciled again. Blass was also with them, and Golo Ganges. I quickly sneaked by the assembled literati. Rudi Kurtz spoke of the wild myth of my *Wupper*. Why did I ever curse him! This is really the limit! I dare anyone to say something nasty about him. Addio!

Today is St. Peter Hille's name-day. A stranger asked me what St. Peter Hille had been like. The questioner was an astronomer and he made the true, shining picture of him. Why I do not make a pilgrimage on his name-day to his grave – had I been Mary or Magdalene – but between us even the intimacy of tears did not exist. I wait respectfully until the prophet appears to me. Just as I wait, as the astronomer said, for the heavenly apparition, so do they wait for the comet. But you didn't know, Herwarth, that St. Peter Hille once met an angel in the field? As he told it to me, his brown eyes became blue, and a blind man, who was listening to our conversation ecstatically confided to me later that he had been able to see while the prophet was telling the story of the angel. It would really be worth something to me if he could hear the melody which you consecrated to his poem; he might have been pleased; and my bible, *Das Peter Hille-Buch*, he might have carried always in the big pocket of his coat, and looked up whatever he might have forgotten about himself. Sometimes he really forgot that he was a prophet. We must build a temple for St. Peter Hille in which to think about him; whose heart would be mighty enough to devote himself entirely to him? Your temple-builderess. Greetings, little Kurt.

The Secessionist-painter Hernstein really believes that he is the bishop. I am myself guilty of having always called him the distinguished Jewish cardinal. In addition, he finds that my correspondence is losing its verve, that it is no longer funny. Yet now I know something funny again. The 'real bishop' asked me whether he might introduce his girlfriend to me. When my inquiries about her financial situation were unappreciated, I replied to my bishop that I could not afford this luxury. I'm really making a sacrifice, my friend, since his giggling blond thinks that I am a rascal, but I cannot meet *everybody* gratis in my unfortunate financial circumstances. Isn't that enough to make you laugh?

Rudolf Kurtz wrote me a letter in the style of Kleist's time this morning. But his lines reveal to me clearly a dissatisfaction, and that is the reason I sent you, somewhat circuitously, the telegram about the Hiller-Hoddis-Kurtz etc. alliance. And for this reason it was kept short, in his own compact style of writing. His last essay (I think in *Die Gegenwart*) was, in content, an intellectual book, exactly two pages long. But because I did this, the reconciliation-telegram was all the more pleasing to Max Fröhlich, dear friends bundled in your fur coats. He paints the way I make poems. For this I love him beyond words; my love also includes his wife, who is a sculptress, did you know that? Oh, his is such a brilliant variety of colors on the bright walls! To think about line there is like trying to trace the outline of solar spots. The radiant imagination of his art casts a range of interacting colors. Kete Parsenow, the Venus of Siam, lies on a silk background, a jewel in the golden frame!

Do you know who suddenly came into the room when Gertrude Barrison was dancing? Minn! But he understands Eastern dance in a way that I don't; I make an exception only of Gertrude. The last beauty of Barrison's dancers moves in an interesting and graceful manner, and her garments are silken secrets of the white-wigged days of the age of the Marquis. All of the on-lookers were charmed.

Today I ran into the bishop on the Spree bridge. I was very pleased by his sudden appearance; all day I had an incomprehensible fear again, and my heart hardly had a beat. And I even saw colors that were not there. I was glad that the bishop offered no pedantic method to calm me down. He possesses a gentle will, which he, like you, Herwarth, can cast over me. Indeed he does not understand that a fluttering dove, standing between antediluvian Mammoths, can be frightened. How did my soul manage to reach the state of touching helplessness? That is, I have noticed that even the most callous person is moved by my fear. Now I often pretend to be afraid when I become too difficult for my own self. And yet I must get some return for my hours of suffering. And we climbed up into the bishop's hermit's garret. On the walls dusty ideas hang, melancholy pictures. I sat myself down in a big chair and tried not to be too relaxed yet, and I observed my savior through half-closed eyes. The bishop's features are made of stone with a warm color, his eyes are hard blue, and his brows sometimes are like steel. He began to caress my hand, he knows that I love tenderness, and I answered with embarrassed coarseness. 'Where are you at the moment?' the bishop asked me. In fact I was sitting at the end of a pot-holed street in Cairo – I am four years old – in a torn smock, a faded fez on my unkempt, shorn head, and my eyes glued together by thousands and thousands of tiny insects. I have so often seen these little troubled children sitting and begging in the ditches of the streets; 'sweet bishop, ever since that time I have often felt like the neglected child of a donkey-driver.' He gave me a coin, it was really a golden penny, a lucky penny; I let it dance on the palm of his hand; there it became a small, glowing ball of earth, until it fell to the ground. Then we kissed, Herwarth; do you think that's bad? I was terribly sorry about it, thought about the many pulsating homelands in life I had left, all of which wore the color of my love. Everywhere a drop of my blood calls me back. Now, however, in the little hermit's cell, on the top floor, I return to myself, unconstrained, I coalesce radiantly. The bishop, of course, thinks (he sometimes forgets his new rank) that he should be punished for kissing me. He thinks you might bring charges against him, and there is a criminal penalty for doing that, he vigorously emphasized, because he apparently feared my frankness. Can you guess my answer? And what of it – ! And just think, Herwarth, I have you to thank for my being able to cool off the situation.

Is it only my imagination – your doctor would like to set a trap for me. And yet I cannot be more candid than in my letters to you and Kurt. But on several occasions an acquaintance of the doctor sat down near my table. That would still not support my suspicion, but the acquaintance looks like a rabbit, and one of his ears is already worn out from eavesdropping. How mystical it is to be respectfully angry with someone. A dead space lies between us, in which nothing more can bloom, but we offer the piety of our friendship at the gravesite – sometimes in the shape of multicolored immortals. Can the doctor at some time have had similar thoughts? No one brings me news of him. It must be like this after death, we have become dependent spirits while still alive. He appears to me often in roles, sometimes as a higher spirit, who says no. As Satan he frightened me recently on the banks of the Spree, when I was secretly waiting for the bishop. He is slender; his shadow like a cameo, he came upon me suddenly in a dream as one of the kings murdered by Richard. Do I resemble in my being a bloodhound? Now is the winter of my discontent – I have even gotten through the awful summers. Your Shakespeare.

DEAR BOTH OF YOU!

In a restaurant on Friedrichstrasse our doctor sat, Herwarth. I only wanted to use the telephone there, but when I noticed him, I slipped out into the gallery and observed him from my perch. He was alone, otherwise there were only bare tables. Then he began to hum again, in a voice that surged against the columns of the room. I don't understand what still keeps him from giving recitals. He is, of course, no folk-singer, like all the twittering, ornate singers, music-making sylvan leaves. The doctor's voice, in places, is unstrung, I can place many of the black pearls in my hand. Wüllner's sounds are all lined up on gold wires, the doctor's oceanic voice should be strung on ropes. His teacher ought to be aware of this. You must disabuse him, Herwarth.

DEAR HERWARTH!

I painted Peter Baum for *Der Sturm*. All summer long he has shown no concern for me, he seems no longer like a great prince, but, as I painted him in his depression, like a rabbit. I showed him his picture, but he refused to pay for the negative plate. Now, with this letter, I turn to his cousin. Please, Herwarth, dot the i's; he is educated, he wrote a mathematical book on births and deaths.

'Honored Sir. Are you the Johannes who is Peter Baum's cousin? I am his friend Amanda and I go to work in the button factory, and am not like those who have gone to the girls' high school in Elberfeld, and High German makes my head itch. You are one of the fashionable people and therefore you correctly spend two thaler for the sketch of your cousin Peter; otherwise there will be no picture of his mug. Peter brought you to my attention in an intimate moment, Mr. Johannes. And I send you friendly greetings and content yourself with one less bulldog, and feed your quails with devil's berries, and drink a glass of wine to my health. Your Amanda Wallbrecker, from Elberfeld Grüne Pumpe an der Klotzbahn 86.'

DEAR BOY!

I waited the whole day for the money-order messenger, afraid that he would take the money to your office. You see, I intend to go to the circus, and a good seat costs three marks; and I want to invite the Slav to go with me, so that he may see that the world has more than cows, for he is obsessed with himself. I am disgusted that people whom I consider to be people are also not people; they strangle love with their ambition. And love, Herwarth, you know what I think of love: if it were a flag I would conquer or die for it. Goodnight.

HERWARTH!

Just think, the two thaler arrived, together with a subscription to *Der Sturm*. See what a wholesaler I am. Hire me, you have never understood business, and I don't want to wait until *Der Sturm* has decimated everything. I have written a bit more to my Peter Baum about his painting:

PITTER!

I never thought that you are such a dummy, no. How can you write me such a silly postcard from Hiddensee! For that you should be punished. I shall bring all your extravagances and hocus-pocus to the attention of your wonderful family and to the *Vorwärts*. I shall also expose your fine brother Hugo. You spend the summer and fall in fine hotels, picking people's pockets while I sit here by the empty cooking-pot. Where did you get all that money? Perhaps from your aunt in the waffle-hut, or from the giant-lady? You have squandered the legacy of your great grandfather, the director of the Olympia flea-circus, to buy yourself new trousers or a Shabbas tablecloth. You stand there exactly like a minister, with a long pipe in your puss, in front of the door of your villa, on the penny postcard, and Hugo looks out the window like your vicar. And an Aeolian harp also stands on the roof; who is playing it? Your loyal Amanda.

DEAR BOYS!

Caius-Maius said to me that he has invited Willi Himmel from Regensburg to the 'Gnu.' The cabaret-evening is taking place in the Café Austria. It would really be nice if Willy Himmel came. He reminds me of the grammar school child whom my oldest sister graciously bequeathed, along with her clothing with their many ribbons, to my second sister, before she retired. He had, like the Regensburg student, big, intelligent eyes, and was no spoil-sport, and he had the exact same name.

I went by car to the cabaret, I really feel sick. 'Gnu' sounds like kangaroo. But it was interesting there, thousands and thousands of people came, wanting to get in, but there was no more room. I climbed up on the stage and sat on a tall chair. With the huge sapphire on my finger (a very large blue piece of glass) I looked like Leo XXVII. Caius-Maius thought so too. The poetry reading soon began.

HERWARTH, LITTLE KURT!

A Zeppelin again passed over our house. I sat asleep at my writing desk when the earth suddenly rolled up – a modern thunder-storm, the world collapses, I have no more time to pack my trunk. A crazy mood in the air; the ocean rushes over our roofs and houses – what has happened to the sky, where is the whale up there going so calmly through the tidal clouds. Adieu, adieu, I'm running swiftly down to the fields. Else.

Today only a few news items!

First: Dr. Alfred Döblin has set himself up as an obstetrician and as a general factotum. The name-plate in Blücherstrasse 18 Hallesches Tor announces that he was the chief doctor at the Urban clinic. What an advertisement!

Second: Leonhard Frank has again painted a girl with a heavenly blue body, now I really believe in his Satanic power!

Third: Scherl wants to employ me to help with the circulation of *Der Gartenlaube* in Tripoli. I shall be living with Enver Bey.

Fourth: The incomparable Baron von Schennis was in the café again yesterday.

Fifth: Poiret has invited all of Berlin's virgins to an audition at Gerson's. They lined up, forming a wall to the left and to the right of the entrance. Between blond and dark women's hair a fissure opened, I saw the model and marveled. She was not born in the city, no one knew where she came from.

Sixth: The café and environs, Berlin and its suburbs, sends its greeting to you gulls!

Just imagine, the *Neue Freie Presse* published a warrant-poster for the arrest of Kokoschka; but he always seemed to work busily, he was always touching when he began to imagine the villa that he would give to his parents. He always had an insatiable appetite for idealistic causes. I really feel sorry for him! Even though he doesn't like me! That's not the way I am! He is supposed to have stolen a model, a wooden little house, at night, between the fifteenth and sixteenth of October. I cut out his picture for you here, it's an amateurish drawing and, to tell the truth, his criminal features have been softened. Has he found a good boarding-house to hide in, one that will take care of him? Rattke, the waiter in the café, at whose place he lived here in Berlin, also hopes that someone is looking after him.

DEAR HERWARTH!

I have sent a manuscript for *Die Fackel* to the Dalai-Lama in Vienna. Here is the copy.

MOST WORTHY DALAI-LAMA, MOST HONORED MINISTER!

I would like to tell you something about heaven, which I dedicate to my mother.

About Heaven

One must seek it in oneself, it blooms best of all in people. And whoever has found it, a most delicate blue wonder, a blessed upward glance, must nourish his celestial bloom. Miracles issue from it; countless miracles yield transcendence. If I could always only be at one with myself, I would like to be the tiller of celestial beds. How one might be reconciled with oneself, and kiss one's own eternity. Would that I had experienced a person as immutably as I have experienced myself! Two knocks on the door, intimate welcome. My thoughts swirl around me, around all life – that is the great journey around all the ringing bells of the heart and whispers, over embankments raised by joy, over sunken depths; and I fall in pits dug by fear – to find again and again one's heart-prints, the pulse of one's blood, until one hears within oneself the first flutter of wings, as one becomes an angel – and looks down on oneself – sweet mysticism. And it is an error to call someone who has received heaven's grace a dreamer, because he wandered through eternity and escaped man, but smiled with God: St. Peter Hille. – What do the wretched people know who never experienced blue at their hearts' goal, or in the course of their dreams in the night. Or those driven from heaven, those who were robbed of blue in their youth. Heaven can no longer find in them light for blossoming. But the doubter spreads paleness, the cultivation of heaven requires strength. For example, the Nazarene, filled with heaven, he spoke, and glowed sumptuously blue, so that his coming was a miracle; he wandered, eternally blue, over the fields of the land. And Buddha, the Indian king's son, carried heaven's flower within himself, in the fulfillments of blue plenitude. And Goethe and Nietzsche (art is speaking with God) and all those who look upwards are graced by heaven and even Heine convinces me, heaven hung above him, and therefore he carelessly tore into the blue divine tendrils, like a wild child tugging his mother's hair. Hauptmann's face and yours also, Dalai-Lama, appear blue. No one can earn heaven falsely, but many pluck the young, celestial flower in man before it is attached firmly. *They are the devils.* Their life is without vision, their hearts without breadth. The Nazarene on the cross also wanted to give to the devil next to him a gentle cloud, a drop of dew from his heaven. But a deaf and dumb person is easier to convince than someone too dumb to have any belief. He sins against himself.

One cannot enter heaven if one does not have it within oneself, only the eternal presses forward towards eternity. Heaven *doesn't* open itself to the heaven-blooming because of their good deeds, nor do their misdeeds damn them to dust. Heaven does not reward or damn. But eternal values determine heaven. It mirrors itself in people, inconceivable, like God himself. Wealthy and thoughtful is the one who carries heaven within himself. The miracles of the prophets, the works of artists, and all enlightenments, as well as the incalculable playfulness in the eye, rise from eternity, the enduring blue of the heart. Sometimes a painful responsibility overcomes me, but one cannot look deeply enough into oneself and look up at heaven.

Divinity in heaven cannot be comprehended, there would soon be nothing left to touch – eternity cannot be curtailed at all. The divinity of heaven in human beings is genius.

Farewell, very honored minister, my heaven does not make me happy in the earthy sense, I cannot share it. But the deepest memories of my blood play wonderfully and repeatedly in the gleam of my blue. Fata-Morgana. Late amazement, blessed upward glance. – Wear the sapphire of my blue evening hours as a memento of your brooding hand.

HERWARTH, LITTLE KURT, COMRADES, BROTHERS!

Did you read in *Pan* Rudolf Kurtz's battle-cry to all theater-directors? He has unleashed a flood over my dried-up *Wupper* – I myself had already given up on it. But now I also carry at my side my velvet sword, which my Negro Tecofi is wearing as a supernumerary in the theater. Wa kadaba kabinahu hinama raga utu dalik, lia nahu jakra anisa a wahalakujunna!!!

Pitter Boom sent me six jars of the honey (by Gühler and Biene) for his picture. I've been humming to myself now all day. No one has heard a word from Kokoschka. In general I am tired of life. Ruth offered to write to Kokoschka for me, because he has such rich patrons. But I know the type and spared her the trouble.

VERY HONORED MR. KOKOSCHKA!

Really I should be angry with you, since you didn't make the slightest effort, after having enjoyed the greatest hospitality in our house, to say goodbye. But one cannot be angry with you. I said that yesterday to Mrs. Lasker-Schüler, who lay in bed, very sick. Write her a line, saying that her picture gave you pleasure – she is such a dear, poor creature and was so crazy about you. Things are not going well for her. She turns down every morsel I give her, she is so stubborn. But couldn't you, in a gentle way, get something for her from your friends? I kindly ask that you be discreet, honored Mr. Kokoschka, for you know how sensitive she is. With best wishes, I remain your Jeptha Elfriede Caro.

INTERNATIONAL POSTCARD

'Don't tell me about Rome –'

DEAR ICE-BUCKETS!

The bishop and I have broken up, he maintains that I misused him. How can one misuse someone else? I should very much like to be on good terms again with him, and ask him himself. Herwarth, write something to him! Mr. Architect Gregor Münster, Hildebrandstrasse 11. – He also wanted to hammer me, I mean in stone al fresco. Perhaps I'll come upon a house someplace. – Yesterday I sat down at his table, he drank brandy and seltzer. I called Otto, who brought me a glass; when I filled it with the strange Syphon, the bishop had to suppress a laugh. But he didn't speak with me. He is a charming teacher. Or he has character; that's what people say when someone keeps his qualities buttoned up within himself. So you can say he is predictable; I'm more aggravating and more difficult. Isn't that more elegant? Or perhaps he only acts that way towards me and follows your tactics, Herwarth, when you play the insulted party. You know, falling out with others is difficult with me. The things one must endure!

Today in the café I was disguised as a bear. An automobile-driver lent me his fur coat. People returning from the theater were sitting in the back room. At the next table senior grammar-school teachers were arguing; would that I were still studying Latin today with Professor Cohn. But in the little corner of the sofa Höxter was asleep, letting the fringes of his hair carelessly hang over his eyes. His old jacket is crumbling, but he wears green silk stockings in patent leather shoes. Next to him Mrs. Spela sat quietly, a secret snail, curled up elegantly. Park atmosphere the color of moonshine. Fritz Lederer-Rübezahl was laughing in the middle of the café, together with his wife, who has a cool, fashionable scent and blue, tulip eyes. And just think, Otto Freundlich is here from Paris because of the New Secession; he entered the café together with Gangolf, who always comes from Italy, whether he arrives from Friedenau or Florence. From time to time I growled at Caius-Maius from my bear-skin. I also saw Pechstein with his Indian girl, and M. Richter with his Roman girlfriend. And many came in and out; finally our dear director Wauer, who recognized me in my get-up, arrived, but I was sweating a whole *Wupper*.

INTERNATIONAL POSTCARD

Don't tell me about Rome!

DEAR HERWARTH AND LITTLE KURT!

Daniel Jesus, the king of Bohemia, is here; I mean Paul Leppin. He has written a new novel, he dedicated it to me; he even wrote from Prague: 'Dear, dear, dear, dear Tino.' Oh, what a lovely salutation, a song. I would like to teach many people to sing like that.

VERY HONORED ENVOY

I, the poetess of Arabia, princess of Baghdad, granddaughter of the sheik, formerly Jussuf of Egypt, interpreter of ears of corn, corn-manager and favorite of the Pharaoh, award the Order of the Elephant with emerald and the black chain with crocodile teeth first-class to the great essayist Rudolf Kurtz.

Cohn is riding, Oesterheld has married a woman, all for my *Wupper*. At the same time Cohn (Oesterheld would have gladly taken my essays) rejected my new manuscript, saying that he can't buy an apple-white horse to go along with his black one. I stood in front of his garden like a rejected traveling salesman with a sample case under his arm. 'One should broil such a fellow alive, or he should break his neck …!' – In any case I sent him in the evening a farewell verse, on which I hope he cut his tongue:

> Rider and royal knight,
> Bitterly, in the storm, I tore into tatters
> In the thorn bush in front of your lattice
> My manuscript.
> Brigitte

Today I received a letter from the Mouse Tower outside Bingen in the morning mail. An admirer of Peter Baum seems to live there. But that person certainly has no sense of humor. This inhabitant of the Mouse-tower asks me whether Mr. Peter Baum really is a loafer, because it is just not congruent with the generosity and aristocratic sensibility of his novels and castle-tales. Because of his appreciative criticism, I answered him: 'Sir, I have no doubt that you are located in the Mouse. Didn't you notice that my Norwegian correspondence is a popular comedy – although with serious outpourings, something like what the storm itself produces. Peter Baum begged me particularly to play the role of loafer in my work, to remain completely unrecognized: I myself, sir, tied a red-patterned handkerchief around his neck, and stuck a brandy-flask in his opened coat-pocket. In real life he is more boring, it pains me to disillusion you; that is, he sits all day up in his room and *works*. I despise that in him, as well as his self-sufficiency, but he is a dear, dear, dear, dear person, as is his Mama; but Johann, his cousin, plays the baron on my revolving stage and his profession is: dogcatcher.'

HURRAH, DEAR HERWARTH, DEAR LITTLE KURT!!! HURRAH!

My twin cousins-Thereses, Therese Tiergarten and Therese Mattaïkirchplatz, sent me a fur coat for Christmas. My most fervent wish. In the summer I am going to pawn it, simply because of the Hugue-moths.

Jakob van Hoddis, the raven, has run off with a dame. During the summer he always sat on the ledge of the front window of Friedländer's, 21 Potsdammerstrasse, hungering, among the towering hats and rose bonnets, for the sweet little Marquise in her little peacock slippers. A soul that was for sale for 60 marks.

HERWARTH!

I believe that I can write no more letters to you. When I sat down outside in front of the café today, a perfect stranger in a threatening coat pounced on me, came up very close to me, nearly knocking over the chairs at my table with his wild gyrations. I heard the man breathing like Karl von Moor: he said that I was an incredible swindler of a woman, that I gave false testimony about myself, that I was blasphemous in my heart – for among the many, many love letters in *Der Sturm*

I was only hiding what was not written. I was too tolerant to tell the man to leave my table, I let him get a lemonade and even placed a cream puff from the dish on his plate. He calmed down but I did not, you two can bet on that, you cool Skagerrak characters. I suddenly hate you, dear, good Herwarth, and you, little Kurt, and all the people in the café as well, and the many people worthy of love and hate in the world. Don't all of you stand like a living wall between them and me. And I also hate the perfect stranger, to whom I dictated my 'unwritten' love letter, until it caught fire under his trembling hand.

Today the bishop came by my place; we whisper more gently each time we meet. My heart is so sensitive; I hear with my heart and gentle speech is so good for us. He sat in my camping-place (you Herwarth, I have put up a tent exactly in the middle of the room) and played with his shell-pencil; I used my huge diamond to draw the moon until it floated away – like this: Between the white night of the paper, all alone, without a star or earth. How frightfully one can draw, but I asked the bishop to use his rushing pencil to place an ocean under the moon. But that's the way it is with me with noses which I draw, or mouths, or half faces; I must complete them, so that they make sense, so they are not without a meaning, and in so doing you often neglect the meaning of yourself, and the heart so seldom loves until the end. Herwarth, you too must learn to whisper, one hears the world's echo very clearly. When the bishop and I whisper, the walls grow quiet and the furniture bearable, its colors mild. And the mirrors of the cupboards are brooks, and our love is a little home or a cricket, a dandelion, out of which children make chains.

DEAR BOYS!

Today I received a postcard from the Rheingold in Berlin:

DEAR, BEST MRS. L.-SCH.!
We all miss you!!! Loos.

DEAR, UNKNOWN LADY!

Mr. Loos has heaped such praise upon you that I almost fear to make your acquaintance. No poetess in all of Germany writes verse equal to that of Mrs. L.-Sch., that is the least of what he says, and then he recites the Tibet-tapestry from morning until evening. But we hope that you are what he says you are. And someday we shall meet. Greetings from Karin Michaelis.

Arnold Schönberg. Webern. Best wishes, Ludwig Kainer. Ada and Emil Nolde. Little Kurt. Best wishes, Albert Ehrenstein. Herwarth Walden. Döblin – as always. Erna Reiss. Gustav Wallascheck. Hede von Trapp. William Wauer. Lene Kainer.

Now when you are both again in Berlin; I completely forgot, have my letters sent back to you from Norway. Else.

The Dalai Lama thinks that some of my models are not sufficiently challenging for my art. I can interpret the minister's words in no other way. But all that matters is what I make of the models. Beyond that I have nothing to do with them. And I shall sell my poetry later, to sell my soul to a publisher, and nevertheless the Dalai-Lama has opened my eyes; since that time I have felt that to be a poetess is to be a pawn-broker; I always, almost without exception, place too high a value on people. O these losses!

DEAR HERWARTH!

Please make the announcement in *Der Sturm* that all members of our communal café who so wish may choose not to be mentioned in letters to you. I grant them free withdrawal.

DEAR HERWARTH AND DEAR KURT!

Sometimes Caius-Maius on the telephone seems like a trumpeting angel, blurting everything out in the twilight. He sits with two wings at his writing-table, while everything flies in his window, as though from the literary land of milk and honey. When he is writing an extraordinary comic poem, I interrupt him with my damned ringing. To do that, I still wear a little bell around my neck. Sometimes I can really be a sheep. Why do I need to ask him whether people like my Norwegian letters? He will always know someone who finds something wrong. Yesterday your frowning doctor complained about my mentioning him in my letters to you. I am flabbergasted by that. Furthermore, a great grandson of Bach wants to take his own life (that's what he promised Caius-Maius) in case I mentioned him in my correspondence. A pity, he has a rosy, glorious smile. He will throw himself into the waves of the holy Franziskus, because a poetess bravely sang him a serenade in the middle of the *Sturm*.

DEAR KURT!

Yesterday he himself threatened me. Is my answer litigation-proof?

SIR!

You want to take your life in case I mention you in *Der Sturm*, or do you plan to suggest it to me indirectly? Especially since you may assume that I am not sentimental, I let everyone follow his own inclinations, in fact the life of such a person doesn't much matter to me. But until now there never was a question of using you as a model either for a portrait or for a caricature. Indeed I have in the past succeeded in creating a word out of a prudish cipher. But be patient, have courage. Deepest respects.

HERWARTH!

Loos is no ordinary gorilla, he is a royal gorilla. He asked me whether he would once again find himself in *Der Sturm*? Did you know that he wears, for the time being, mutton chops on his cheeks; that has a mollifying effect, improving the pure features of his face. Most men wear branching beards to indicate their manliness, or to obscure their broad mouths or long chins. Adolf Loos told me stories from the African forests, his eyes shone with earnest gracefulness. O, he is kind, and that is a divine quality, the highest thing one can say about a person.

DEAR CHILDREN!

I have answered Karin Michaelis:

KARIN

First I cast a little star into the K of your first name and greet you! Your books are variegated doves; white, blue, but also red, demonic doves, and golden and silver whirlwind doves are among them. For this reason I do not place your books in the cage of the book case. Tino of Bagdhad.

HERWARTH!

You can publish the following in *Der Sturm*:

Under the blind cover of Heinrich Mann the abbé Max Oppenheimer delivered the blood of Kokoschka to Munich's critics.

Abbé painter Oppenheimer must have received my lines today:

DEAR MAX OPPENHEIMER!

Unlike the narrow-minded general public, I have always taken pleasure in your ostentatious clothing. It shows not only courage but also good taste. I went very eagerly with you to Munich to your exhibition, though your pictures were not hanging on the walls but only those of Oskar Kokoschka. And you had to take me, of all people, who knows your original, there with you. Did you consider me so uncritical – do you belong to the group of people who are accustomed to take on the words and gestures of a second person, with whom you are in love? You are, I assume, in love with Kokoschka and your pictures are plucked works, for that reason they lack roots. And yet you possess your own garden. The picture of Heinrich Mann gave me exceptional pleasure, like a shining copy, and I saw in its colors and rhythms the painter Oskar Kokoschka, not you. Is there something of Max Oppenheimer in Kokoschka's pictures? In the old museums people actually copy the old masters, but do not put their names at the bottom. Kokoschka is an old master, born later, a terrifying wonder. And I make no allowances in matters of eternity, you should also be more pious in respect to time. Otherwise I am, as always, trust me, well disposed towards you, Max Oppenheimer, dear abbé.

7 December 1911

Else Lasker-Schüler

Who doubts his originality? He gladly assumes his original shape as a coarse angel.

Today I went, together with my maid, through Friedrichsruherpeterbaumstrasse in Halensee along the railway tracks. My maid is my half-price Sunday-gallery audience. Walking alongside her, I can never really enjoy my thoughts, nor sink into despair about them; she always drives out my inspirations. Because she only acts that way, in reality everything bores her, but she has grown accustomed to the rhythm of the railroad tracks of my language, even with its difficulties; sometimes she is derailed, but she always gets past me to her treasure. I like very much to look at some people as the divine works of ancient domes and temples. 'Only St. Peter Hille could not be looked at, he was invisible, he was a sun who did the looking.' My narration is straightforward, I spoke as though to a child, and yet since then I have felt embarrassment in the presence of the creature, just the way I felt ashamed in school of my most beautiful gifts; the world is filled with servant girls and slaves (of poor and rich, of the trained and the ignorant); the German always confuses coarseness with originality; and yet a potato tuber would understand me better than a coarse person. I hate love among ordinary people; if the prophet were still alive, I would write him a pastoral letter, that he forbid love. St. Peter Hille was an aesthete. Tristan and Isolde needed to love each other, Carmen and Escamillo, Ratcliff and Mary, Sappho and Aphrodite, the moor of Venice and Desdemona, Wilhelm von Kevlaar, you, Herwarth, and Gretchen, Romeo and Juliet, Faust and Margaret, Mephisto and the Venus of Siam, the white panther and Joseph of Egypt, Sascha the imprisoned prince and Scheherazade – 'he' named me Scheherazade. Good night.

DEAR CHILDREN!

Today the sculptor Georg Koch visited me and brought me chocolate bonbons. I ate up all the sweet things with Marzipan and sugar fillings, one after another. They were wrapped in silver-green paper with gold stars. I played the whole night with them; first I put on a coat made out of the enchanted fairy-tale radiance, then my feet stood in silver-green shoes with stars, a crown glowed in my hair; I sat suddenly in a circus with Lorchen Hundertmarck, who was allowed to accompany me – the little daughter of the coachman – her father drives the carriages of my beloved aunt Johanna. Lorchen and I are both ten years old and yearn secretly for Joy Hodgini; we poke each other in the ribs, no one was listening, they were all looking into the large, round arena, and many hands were clapping. Lieschen Hundertmarck has a bureau on which stands: a little sea-shell chest, in its mirror a golden porcelain angel stares from its pedestal; a small blue glass lamp with a yellow ribbed Christmas candles, and a wax heart lies on a card next to a gleaming Easter-egg. When you look at it you can see a fairy-kingdom. Next to it lies a prayer book, made of green velvet; from the prayer book hangs a bookmark made of silver-green shining foil with golden stars.

Are you aware, Herwarth, that Paul Zech from Elberfeld is moving to Berlin? I advised him to make this move, he really doesn't have to send you his verses always. From his last poems chimneys smoke, rust lies on every word. He is the only regional poet of note.

DEAR HERWARTH!

This evening I had another crazy dream, I was strolling across the Kurfürstendamm, dressed like a tramp, in tattered pants and worn-out skirt, thinking only dull thoughts, and I was also tipsy – out of sadness. – The wind was howling against my red nose. But you've seen this before in me, but not as bad – when you had gone on a trip and returned, and found me up here in Henriettenplatz, as if I were homeless. This time, in the dream, Kete Parsenow, the Venus of Siam, came up to me. After searching for some words, she grasped me by the elbow with her ivory hands, but with the energy of a policeman – 'Tino!'

HERWARTH, LITTLE KURT!

I always forget his name – he is from the Tirolian area of Saxony, he wrote a book about painted terra cotta pots, the future director of the museums here. I don't know anything more about him. Incidentally, he owns his own furniture, inherited from his great aunt; and he has a country cousin of the Mona Lisa hanging on the tapestry, the painting he also inherited from his arch-aunt Isabella.

DEAR BOYS!

Why do you never ask me what I meant by the mysterious 'Don't tell me about Rome?' I wanted, you see, to open a fortune-telling salon called 'Don't tell me about Rome?' – but since both of you have passed over it in silence, how could strangers be taken in? I'd do better as a peddler.

Just think, Herwarth, our Rosa just came and gave me notice; must I now leave the house or she? She secretly subscribed to *Der Sturm* via Leipzig, and took offense at the account of the walk with me through Friedrichsruherpeterbaumstrasse. Her sense of honor has been attacked; she feels hurt, I must now clean my house myself or not clean it. I have become dust among dust. Her Willy would not now marry her, what do you think if I promise her to hold the marriage ceremony at our place?

DEAR BOTH OF YOU!

Peter Baum seems in bad shape; he longs for Elberfeld, he even thinks of his wet-nurse with great affection. Her carries her on his watch chain in a heart-envelope. She nursed his ancestors, and comes from Remscheid. She was the one who really started him on verse, right?

DEAR TRAVELERS!

I have printed, once and for all, in hieroglyphic writing, an answer to the many letters I receive, for each letter, from whomever it may come. 'Go take a flying leap!' What will Richard Weiss and Paul Leppin in Prague, both of them, whom I like so much, say to this discourtesy! Such a discourtesy can really become a compulsion, it then takes the shape of an enemy that clearly creates enemies. Suppose that the Venus of Siam writes a letter to me in the next few days and I send an answer back to her in hieroglyphics. Or Ramsenith? Do you know who Ramsenith is – he has been living in Munich since the Testament and wears a pyramid on his head and is lovely, his eyes reach into heaven. He is the only person who can prove historically that I am Jussuf the Egyptian, for I lived at his court.

DEAR HERWARTH!

My heart is very sick, or does it feel excessively large? If it spills over, one always trivializes the feeling by imagining that one is merely sick. That is picked up from doctors. Herwarth, yesterday evening my heart was granite red, I could hear, taste the color in my mouth. My heart was the sunset, and sank. Outdoors, in this dismal winter-time, it can no longer happen; I died of sunset. Can you understand, could anyone ever understand, when I spoke of the stars as though they were my brothers, accompanied through the clouds by the moon, a jolly, disarming gentleman, Berncastle Doktor, old Valerian noble vintage? O, I am not joking, I do not wish to amuse both of you, but to rescue myself continually with games like those Till Eulenspiegel played. I would have become a clown, Herwarth, if it would not have offended you.

INTERNATIONAL POSTCARD

Dear Herwarth, I am very sad, I hear weeping all day long in the city. – But as I turned around, it was me. I weep, Herwarth, because someone is angry at me.

GOOD CHILDREN!

I am deeply moved, my soul has melted, emerald and ruby and sapphire pour down it, as well as moonstone, like multi-colored springs. And I always speak two words, the title of my singed, 'unwritten' love-letter, which was addressed to Sascha at Saint Petersburg citadel: Heavenly prince

I no longer have a secret; my heart cannot keep one, my heart lies open to the world. Oceans come and pour the secrets of the heart onto the land, it awakens at daybreak and dies at sunset. But my heart is still made of silk, I can close it like a case. Do you know a secret, or ask little Kurt, that would be worthy of my discretion?

DEAR HERWARTH, DEAR LITTLE KURT!

Did I really mix up the letters yesterday, sending Peter Baum's letter to you, and your letter to Peter Baum? Or did the post office play a trick, the postal clerk with the goatee always looks at me like a faun.

PITTER!

When you receive this letter I shall have killed myself, but you need not concern yourself with it. Peter, this time I really have fallen head over heels in love, guess with whom! You no longer believe me, Peter, but it is really true, and I can no longer go to work in the factory. Peter Baum, in the morning the boss dismissed me, because I was always gazing into the air, like a pigeon in the pigeon-coop, or sewing the buttons onto the wrong side. And I can no longer eat, and I always hide my heart's painful love in my checkered pillow; or I look at the pictures on the walls, our picture, where we were confirmed, among the rich children. Do you still remember it? How you have changed, Peter, and I too; in times of joy and sorrow we have always remained faithful to one another, and you know quite well that I always came honestly to you, confessing everything to you. 'Work makes life sweet,' Pastor Krummacher once wrote in your poetry album, and he had harsh words for me, because I always laughed under my desk during confirmation class. For you that's all gone now, but I am no longer laughing; now I always want to weep when I think of him. Do you know 'Him?' You know him! Guess! 'Him' and don't tattle to Herwarth, Pitter, and greetings

from your friend, Amanda.

Unhappy Herwarth, Peter has also sent back the letter that I wrote to you. Dear, good Herwarth, remain calm and in good cheer up there on the ice. You will come back home all the more refreshed. But you know me, you cannot rest easy, in any event, I am home all day long and I'm decorating the Xmas tree and in the evening I light the candles and sing songs, sometimes ecstatic, sometimes in the depths of despair. I am wildly happy. From that you can see how loyal I am to you. Say hello to little Kurt, our angel.

Else.

HERWARTH!

So that you know, today I ran, like a school-child, to Jeptha Elfriede – I wanted to unburden my heart to a 'woman.' But she no longer believes me, not until I come to her four weeks from now with the same feeling for 'him.' Please mark the date, you and little Kurt, it was yesterday, December 19. I am totally convinced that my heart is not betraying me, I can rely basically on my heart, but if it deserts me, then I shall become shallow.

I have written to Tristan: Sweet Tristan, at night all my ancestors gather in my tent, Califs and Dervishes and Pashas in lofty turbans. And also a Chief, who taught me how to dance over the bodies of unbelievers, and is now threatening me with the anger of Allah. Tristan, you are an unbeliever, but I love you Tristan, and with the gold of your hair I dazzle the eye of the lord in the Koran. And my palaces and my herds of dromedaries I give to you, they will bow down, shaggy slaves, before you, when you wish to mount them. And you will wear around your neck the strings of my wild blue pearls, and take my ring with the pearl of the Flood. And I give you my heart, you can take it in your hand and play with it. The burning thorn-bush of the sacred mountain and the night and its unspeakable stars are reflected in it. I love you, Tristan.

Tino of Baghdad.

DEAR HERWARTH AND DEAR LITTLE KURT!

Your card showed me that a card can smile ironically; a certain fatherly gaze emanates from the serene, temperate letters, as if they were the hairs of an old man. You must have written it together, right? Serenity must be extremely difficult, at least for me. Your handwriting, Herwarth, is normally a symphonic concert or a pantomime, and little Kurt offers a self-portrait, each hair-stroke of his lines reveals himself. More than anything, I find you both so impudent, to behave so patronizingly towards my confession.

Else.

DEAR HERWARTH!

Tristan too will not believe me that I love him, but he was very gentle when we met; we went hand-in-hand, and he told me the story of the wolf, without knowing that the story is an actual event. I myself was the boy who cried breathlessly through the city, 'The wolf is here, the wolf is here!' And twice I howled to the people, roused fear in them, and when the wolf really did break out of a zoo, no one would believe me. 'He' also will not believe me that I love him, and I shall be devoured by sorrow, and certainly the whole city as well.

HERWARTH!

Please have these poems printed in *Der Sturm*, they are to Tristan – perhaps he will believe then – we cannot lie in a poem.

When we look at each other
Our eyes bloom.

And how astonished we are
At the sight of our miracles – isn't that so?
And everything becomes so sweet.

We are framed by the stars
and we flee the world.

I believe we are angels.

*

The stars in the night
Settle on your blue soul.

We must be quiet with you,
O you, my temple,
My prayers frighten you;

My pearls awaken
From my sacred dance.

There is no day and no star,
I no longer know the world,
Only you – everything is sky.

The sun is no more,
But your face shines.

And the night without miracle,
You are my slumber.

Your eye flashes like a shooting star –
I always desire something for myself.

Your laughter is pure gold,
My heart is dancing in the sky.

If a cloud comes –
I die.

*

I can no longer sleep,
You constantly sprinkle gold over me.

And my ear is a bell.
In whom do you confide?

The bushes in the sky gloom
As brightly as you.

Angels gather your smile
And give it to children.

They play with it as though it were the sun,
Yes ..

HERWARTH!

Tristan has told me that he has a girlfriend, I shall speak no more about him –

I frequently go into the city alone these days, travel with all the moles in the subway. My skin color is like earth now. I must look bad. Can you imagine that somebody said to me that it was just hypochondria! But then it occurs to me that it's normal for one person to ask another: 'how are you?' But I am always looking for the hypochondriac, earth-colored line in my face – along the tracks at the Knie-Görlitzer station. But people by nature have such calcified faces, eggs; Easter eggs at best; I am always glad to find a laughing poster in the lower entrance of the elevated train. The wild little rascal drawn by his father, Ludwig Kainer, I recognized it immediately, in the morning, bravely riding astride the large hand of his servant girl, he laughs at me from the newspaper, as though coming out of a stable. I would like to bring to the least of the Secessionist-painters a green little dwarf horse, it would have to be like a tree, so green and sparkling; that would be the jolliest thing that I could imagine. For a long time now nature has been growing on the asphalt table of the city; the strong, hard heart of Berlin is moving. The fragrance of fir trees colors the blood in the veins and faces seem fresher. But what has that to do with me, I am no longer interested in the fate of this world, I still dream only of the poorest trinkets, glass balls in all the gentlest colors, many formed like little altars, hidden in their niche, gleaming flowers of Mary glow. I believe I can already detect the glassy flowers in my breast. This revelation! And I am not even a Christian; how could I become a Christian? That would mean to disown one's own blood. This recognition should be the proudest wealth of Jehovah's people.

Gulliver built a city here; he is, after all, the architect; Adolf Loos told that to me. Thousands of dwarves, big as matchsticks, tramp through the streets, across the market-place of Midget-town. There were five of us giants and we were very ashamed of our size – and we moved cautiously, bent over. And still we had bad luck; one of us, the actor Murnau, crushed a dwarf. Did you read about it? And Peter Baum, absorbed in thought, put a fireman, ten centimeters tall, in his pocket. The place is just filled with detectives and policemen running around. Caius-Maius, that is, Dr. Hiller, looked like a good-natured cannibal, with his round belly. And Hans Ehrenbaum-Degele invited the dwarves to drink from the New Year's eve punch bowl; I believe he wants to pour them into it.

HERWARTH AND LITTLE KURT!

You know Chamay Pinsky, of course; he has gone with Beate to Jerusalem, to leaven the land. The rascal! He certainly knows that promised people belong to a promised land.

And not Jewish bourgeois, who move from Berlin-Posen to the land of kings; their piety consists of crumbling matzos, strong meat soup. For forty years Moses taught his people the freedom of the desert, and the roar of the jackal, and to read the law from the divine countenance before he led them through Jerusalem's gate.

I think much about religion now, but a world is a part of religion: to be alone. It is not an idyll in a quiet house. I was destined to perform temple-duty, I would have plucked saints from the banks of gentle streams. And I would have kept the light of the soul blue.

I also place *pious images* among the stars that hover above the holiest of the holy, and I always would have known how to kneel before God, so that he would not unleash his rage. I say *du* to God, they are on first name terms with him.

DEAR HERWARTH AND DEAR LITTLE KURT!

There must be a reason for the religious mood I'm in. Do you think that remorse is bothering me? Sin has appeared to me, you think, with purgatory in its hand, or the snake has finally won influence over me. The devil! You believe that I might build a religious feeling on posts set up in the Flood? I have faith both in my good and in my bad acts. I have no sins, though I often try to tempt them with sweets, I have never noticed myself doing that. I live life like a picture, in which I am always present. Sometimes the picture is hung to my disadvantage, or something moves in my setting, or I am not pleased with the frame. Frames are restrictions, non-art, borders, which no god, but a dilettante-God lays out. Round frames still have something circular, but the four-cornered ones, which are now the fashion, have, in such a completely human way, stepped out of the universe. Thus I look out of the picture at life; which of them do I take more seriously? Both. In life I perish, and in the picture breathe again. Hurrah!

DEAR NORTHERNERS!

Suddenly I feel grey, like the day; night is near; should I remain awake or go to sleep? Is it better to live or to miss the chance. Everything should be worth something, even what is not present. I know that somewhere a Hadrian or a Pharaoh longs for me. Now is that true or false? But I find that such a thought is rewarding. However, the burger loses nothing by having such a thought, but it might cost me my life. Do you think that my life is exchangeable? Would it pay me to exchange my life? I want you to answer this thought. But I spoke of Hadrian, I spoke of the Egyptian king who wore a pyramid as a crown, we ride together into battle on dromedaries. I rode behind him, up against his back, and my arrows fly past his heart, into the bodies of the enemy. At night he adorns my lips with his kisses.

HERWARTH!

Karl Kraus, the Dalai Lama, is staying in Vienna, but his hand, cast in marble, hangs downstairs in your studio. I stood again in front of the black board, upon which it is fastened, reaching downwards; it moved, as though wanting to explain something to me. This hand, the confident hand of a minister, the gentle hand of a diplomat, a flickering hand, which can set fire to a city. My eyes dance a polka around its edge. I would much prefer to wrestle with this hand to pass the time of day. Suppose that this noble battle never takes place! During the night I often dream of the battle of our hands, and am astonished that in the morning you always find his still hanging on the board. Recently it has even been smiling. The minister's hand, a serious, Mongolian umbel, a hand in which everyone ends his journey. What does he think then about my aimless hand, fashioned out of play and blood?

DEAR HERWARTH!

What sort of vain competition is life when compared to ascending toward eternity? I am excited, at times today I already had the feeling I must die. Even if I live in a picture, am the picture, my growing eclipse in your eyes has been causing me great pain now for some time. We can scarcely see each other any longer, Herwarth; all the people who want to bring us together again are no more than retouchers, or paint-restorers, they want to freshen us up, to smear false, forced colors over the genuine colors. Forgery! Fake resurrection! Instead, one should embalm people over whom night falls. Today there was a knocking at my door several times, something terrible is happening in the world, pure counterfeit; for such things people spend their money. I tell you this, I wish I owned a bridge; everyone would have to pay me a toll – bridge-toll. Because I am dead, I have decided at least to become rich.

HERWARTH!

First, I am sending you another poem for *Der Sturm*. I am wildly in love with someone, but I'll say no more about it. That way, it *could* always be addressed to you.

> You are everything that is made out of gold
> In the great world.
>
> I seek your stars
> And don't want to sleep.
>
> We shall lie down behind hedges
> Never to arise.
>
> Out of our hands
> Kiss sweet reveries.
>
> My heart fetches
> Roses from your mouth.
>
> My eyes worship you,
> You try to catch their butterflies.
>
> What should I do,
> If you are not there.
>
> From my lids
> Black snow drops;

When I am dead,
Play with my soul.

I have sent Ludwig Ullman the poem: 'To Someone' – for his leaflet:

DEAR LUDWIG ULLMANN!

It was night when your letter arrived; I had just hanged myself, only in the morning I could not find the tree again. Whether that will help your leaflet I cannot judge. For I am still very shaken by the hanging and by everything associated with it. Cheer people up for me, I can't. Berlin is also so boring, neither living nor dying is of any interest, as far as I can tell. Your postcard was refreshing, written in such a lively way; your writing is like well-water, undiluted. You should always write about forests, that would be your strength. In any case, come with me to the Prater when I come to Vienna. Your E.L.Sch.

DEAR BOYS!

I intend to become reigning prince. Wouldn't everyone have to pay me tribute? Yesterday I wrote, unfortunately to no avail, to medical doctor F.:

SIRE!

You have correctly sensed that I am the Prince of Thebes. You want to present me with a blade as a gift. I ask you to enclose two hundred pieces of silver, that is, two hundred German marks, so that I can pay your servant the reward that is owed to him.

Could I have shown greater respect to his master? I had confidence that this doctor would treat my letter respectfully; he is a kidney specialist, has something of the Bohemian about him, and specializes in floating kidneys.

Just now a woman came from Prague, asking me to speak to her group. Since I write so much gratis, I must now double my price for speaking. Willy Haas sent her to my place from Prague. I asked for a thousand marks; two hundred marks for my love poems in particular. The woman was shocked, but she will speak to her group about my price. I was also expressly pompous, wearing my royal cloak sometimes over my shoulders in folds, in crazy folds. In any event, I no longer speak without being paid, only conjunctions; would that I might find one that would bind me together.

HERWARTH!

Ludwig Kainer wants to illustrate my Calif-stories. But we cannot talk here, whether I tell him about the face of my father Mohammed Pasha or Ached the Calif, or about the Fakir, there is always someone else that shows up; that's how many acquaintances we have in Berlin. And neither can I invite anyone to my place; letters to you in Norway, a foot high, lie everywhere. But my distinguished illustrator is going to Munich, I too am going for a few days; by the way, my friend

Antoni, the prince of Poland, wrote from Munich, saying that yesterday my ghost appeared to everyone in the Café Bauer in Galla. I was always curious to get acquainted with my ghost, my astral body; it must be rich, I shall put the touch on it.

'Prince of Thebes,' the painter Schmidt-Rottluff wrote to me, 'I want to paint you with your black servant Ossman.' I wish he would paint me right into the background of his manuscript. Nothing but snake grottoes, jungle vegetation, palm trees, the bodies of apes as big as people. One cannot see through his handwriting into the distance, one suffocates in the writing. He and Richard Dehmel drink out of the same dark springs. I shall tell him stories of my life. But you know that my primeval jungle ancestor is the only person who does not descend from apes. I still have our genealogical tree in bloom. You won't believe it, but the painter with the terrifying handwriting will believe me, that I am descended from the pineapple. O, this intoxicating, wild head of fruit, the chieftain's ornamental bonnet! I have never eaten one, not once nibbled at it, because of my piety, and yet I could devour my vegetable ancestry, like a cannibal.

HERWARTH!

You already know that Ludwig Cranach has painted the Venus of Siam as Kete Parsenow. Then I am not alone in knowing that Kete Parsenow is Venus, the true Venus. I saw Venus smile, I looked at myself in the mirror of Venus' tears, I saw Venus dance, I saw Venus die. I, I, I, I can scarcely touch myself anymore I am so sweet.

DEAR HERWARTH!

Little Paul has made up his mind not to go to the movies anymore, he could not sleep through the night, someone in the film went crazy and none of his little friends wants to go back there anymore. As a rule he likes to watch disasters. He was still very much excited in the morning, and told me the following: there was a man named Marius, who won a girlfriend at a dance, and then the girlfriend wrote to Marius that a window shining in the night would show him where she was. In the same house was a hotel, in fact the house was effectively a hotel; in the front was Doctor Russel's madhouse for the mentally ill; Doctor Russel cures people with rays. Mr. Marius got lost in the dark and entered a cell in the madhouse. A mentally ill man suddenly arrives in an automobile, and one of the attendants puts him to sleep with radiation, and he sleeps. Then he regained consciousness and tried to climb through the window, but he falls down in front of the bed, and Marius suddenly comes in and sees the madman and, terrified, he wants to run behind the wall, but the sick man grabs him by the throat and almost chokes him to death, but not quite; suddenly an attendant, making his rounds, hears this and opens the door, and suddenly one can see into the room of Dr. Russel, who is sitting on the bed, flirting with Marius' girlfriend.

DEAR LITTLE KURT!

Tomorrow I'm coming to your office, 45 Potsdamerstrasse, with the bill for the negative of your picture – I hope you feel that it looks like you.

NOTA:

Negative six marks. 22 marks for the car to get the negative from the factory; 53 marks, *with tip*, for dinner at Kempinski's and for 50 cents of Fachinger. At Kranzler's I drank chocolate for 50 cents and ate, for 75 cents, small, stale tortes. Then took a car back to *Große Rosinen*. (Meinhard played wonderfully.) 30 cloak room, 60 lobby (salmon canapés). Then took an auto, sped off to the Café des Westens, to pick up you and Herwarth; didn't find you, finally returned home in the car, but got back too late, had to roust the concierge from his bed, 25 cents. Please count it all up, make no mistakes. Pamper your painting, but to hell with you. Greetings! Else L.-Sch.

DEAR HERWARTH, DEAR LITTLE KURT!

I met Adolf Lantz; he wears, since he became director, a stove-pipe hat, which is smoking.

I seldom go to the café these days, I know it by heart by now. It's not too difficult to learn; international cafés are harder to keep in mind. I am chattering again to myself, as though withered. I have surrendered everything to time, like a rash ascetic, now the wind takes with it my last, autumn-colored words. Soon I shall be completely empty, completely white snow that fell in Asia. The earth has never been as cold as I am; is there anything else I could die of! I have blown away and disappeared, no one can build a temple out of my bones anymore. I could scarcely remember myself any longer if the winds did not whistle in my face. O, you world, you labyrinth, I no longer care for your fragrance, which makes false dreams grow. You unmasked, frightful prophetess, I have torn the mask from your face. What business have I to be down here, where no star hangs. I am now entirely dependent on my soul, and have tread upon my shores with fear. So much wilderness! I shall be devoured by myself. I celebrate bloody pagan rites, wear the masks of evil animals, and dance with human bones, with your thighs. I must have patience. *I* have patience with myself.

Schmidt-Rottluff painted me sitting in a tent. A mandrill who composes battle-songs, Schmidt-Rottluff has painted me as a mandrill, and I descend from the pineapple. You have overcome the ape; but one can in no way evade the circumstances of one's birth.

Am enchanted with my colorful personality, my ancient fearfulness, my dangerousness, but my golden forehead, my golden eyelids, which watch over my blue composing. My mouth is as red as berries in a thicket, in my cheeks the sky ornaments itself in a blue dance, but my nose quivers toward the east, a battle-flag, and my chin is a spear, a poisoned spear. Thus I sing my solemn song. O, Herwarth, you cannot understand how it feels at all – what remains of the ape in you? Herwarth, you need not repeat this, Herwarth, I swear to you by the prophet Darwin, I am my only immortal love.

DEAR HERWARTH!

I hear that you are holding a musical performance at Caius-Maius in the cabaret Gnu. I still don't know whether I can come. The Gnu has had such a big litter and they certainly won't remain blind to your music. Someone has spread the word that, from time to time you have dedicated one of your songs to someone other than me; your music no longer interests me. There is some truth to that. I always believed that you only could bear my luster, that no pale longing inhered in you.

DEAR HERWARTH!

But I am still going to the cabaret of Dr. Hiller, if only to bring pralines to little Martha Felchow. She sits at the entrance between Prolet and Gnu, and still takes tolls.

I hear that Ludwig Hardt has again performed wonderfully in Choralion hall – he is the only interpreter of Liliencron. Once he gave a Liliencron-evening for me alone, in one of the corners of the café. His performance captured the gentle soul of Liliencron, the steel of his heart. Ludwig Hardt's voice marches with spurs through the poet's war poems. Ludwig Hardt is a lyrical soldier, he is noble, like Liliencron. His parents' home, a lioness, is on a gold chain.

Today Ludwig Kainer is coming to draw me as the Prince of Thebes for *Der Sturm*. My two negroes, Ossman and Tecoñ, the chief's son, will receive him in the courtyard of my palace. I am wearing my holiday outfit and my belt of shells, with the Islamic star of the sultan over my heart, and I shall resemble 'him.'

DEAR HERWARTH, DEAR LITTLE KURT!

I intend to arrange a big celebration; my rooms are not big enough, and this morning I went to the new area of the castle of the marquise Auguste Fürst-Foerster, whose Valencienne hand I respectfully kissed. She was her usual supremely graceful self, and, at my request, placed her salon at my disposal. Her hope also to be permitted to appear at my celebration pleased her no end. Then she accompanied me through the rose tapestries of her corridors; 'Your highness, marquise.' – Marquise (smiling graciously at me): 'Highness' …

HERWARTH!

I have found another drawing of S. Lubinski, which I drew secretly while peering over everybody's heads in the café, because we had fought earlier. He was a character. The only quality which can create a full character is courage. Thus he was even more than a character, he was a rusty structure.

HERWARTH!

Here is an open letter I am writing to Paul Cassirer.

SIR!

It was no surprise to me to admire the works of Oskar Kokoschka in your fine salon. Some of the observers certainly suppressed their smiles, out of respect for you, sir, because of their unshakable belief in you, in your reputation for understanding art, because of your reliable judgment about colors and values and the nature of our time; on the day that you displayed Oskar Kokoschka in your salons you advanced yourself 100 years into the future, since you, as Berlin's leading dealer in art, recognized the eternal value of what he has created. I heard with no less astonishment that you want to arrange in your salons a second exhibition of Kokoschka, that is, of copies of his genius. But why in his own lifetime? Should one dilute pure wine just because it gives people with weak constitutions heart palpitations! Or makes them get drunk, or stagger or become animated. I ask you, with all due respect, sir, to cancel this exhibition. Oskar Kokoschka is no one's twin, he doesn't even have a cousin, only a treacherous friend. Sir, I and the true admirers of the paintings of Oskar Kokoschka are counting on you to cancel an exhibition of copies that a certain someone plans to put on in your salons. With the greatest respect and warmest regards, sir.

Else Lasker-Schüler

Oppenheimer also has hangers-on – yes, indeed –, hanging from his watch-chain.

MAX OPPENHEIMER, ABBÉ!

You want to push me back into the confessional … For no one knows as well as I do, that you write out phony checks with the signature of Oskar Kokoschka. Why? Because you yourself know how to paint.

(I am writing this to him in the café; he believes that I, the Prince of Thebes, am the tool of a faction.)

DEAR HERWARTH!

I wrote to Dr. Hiller:

At lunch today I ate the first-born, not the lentils, but the fat peas. Crumbs were swimming in it, and the remains of a pig's ear. I'm very bloated, but your face, Caius, has become as round as the moon. How dare you permit yourself to address us, above all me, as idiots in your talk; especially since you know I am an idiot. But you need not remind me of it, that is indelicate, that is outright vulgarity on your part. I shall no longer come to the Gnu. I've had enough.

HERWARTH!

Yesterday my uncle, the southern German minister, went to the Russian ballet with me. Behind us sat striking women from St. Petersburg, between them Mr. Barchan, the sorcerer. Several times at our place he conjured up fresh fish, which he then swallowed live; he had wanted to make you too disappear, do you still remember that? I mean, to deny your existence, but his sleeve was not wide enough. I have been writing Norwegian letters for three months now, or longer. Aren't you two going away again soon? Perhaps a second trip, like your trip to the North Pole, will inspire me. I have forgotten how to write in sunlight; my stories of ancestors demand the

East. I have also strapped skates onto my narrative style, and have simply swept it away, I didn't care where it was going. Thus I wrote the greatest part of my letters with my big toe; but one can write history only with one's heart; the heart is emperor. With what do I actually write my poems? What do you believe? I write it with my most invisible design, with the hand of my soul, with my wing. Is it there – certainly. But clipped by malicious life. (Mysticism.)

DEAR HERWARTH!

Moreover, I have drawn the director of the Gnu, Caius-Maius = Dr. Hiller, sitting at the lecture table on the stage. He is speaking about the dappled moon-gnu-calf – because of the noise I understand only half of what he is saying – in his brain – the bulb is reflected electrically.

O, HERWARTH, O, LITTLE KURT!

How the world has changed; in earlier times the night was black, now it is gold-blond.

DEAR LITTLE KURT!

Do you already know that one of your clients has bought *Der Sturm*, and is having her bedroom papered with your picture! She sings: 'I have seen your picture in *Der Sturm*!'

BOYS!

Now I found out the secret about the arts: one must draw the way one performs an operation. Whether one slices off too much or draws a stroke longer is not at all the point! – and the mass appeal of music has become clear to me. The tongue has the most to do while listening, it grows, so to speak, towards listening, it does the tasting; patriotic music pleases it: especially *Deutschland, Deutschland über alles*, folk songs, stirring songs from operettas; *Carmen*, brilliant wedding meal; Wagner's holy grail as well is not to be despised. Your music, Herwarth, of dances and swords, spring and shepherds, moon and night and stars, the crowd gobbles up for turtle soup and Indian bird's nests – *I hope!*

In the evening I now drink Chambard tea, a drink made out of golden chamomile, bluebell flowers, and rose leaves. I have written the fragrant recipe to Peter Altenberg, for another chapter of his book, *Prodromus*. I hear he spits on my fine poem, on my old Tibetan tapestry, as a result it can only become more antique and more valuable.

Peter Altenberger, the poet of Austria, hurrah!!!

DEAR HERWARTH!

When I meet Professor Herrmann, low-hanging clouds come to mind; when I think of Julius Hart, I know where I once met angels. Max Herrmann and Julius Hart are souls intertwined (away with all confetti brains).

DEAR HERWARTH, DEAR LITTLE KURT!

I have given away both my rings; I am sorry, but I have had a large, brown glass beetle mounted in brass; it sits on my middle finger as though on a bare branch in autumn, longing for summer and sun, for flowers and silver leaves, and probably for a glowworm.

HERWARTH!

We are only on the way; life is only a path, has no arrival, for it comes from nowhere. Where should one go? Always to flee into oneself. That is why people are so poor, their hearts offer refuge, they feel secure in their human habitations. Where should one go? My heart has disintegrated; o, this isolation among broken columns! Do you know of a heart bathed in pleasure, even if it is made of marble?

MY DEAR ONES!

I have become very curious; I begin to ask whether I am an intellectual or dull? Sometimes I think something that surpasses my limits; I have already thought much about your horizons in thought. But how can I get anywhere when I hang over my walls and fences, when land has not yet separated from sea? Who will be my creator? Shall I love my creator, or worship him respectfully?

When I'm seriously ill, I don't go for a doctor, Herwarth, but an astronomer, an astrologer or a fakir, or, as far as I'm concerned, a juggler would do. The latter can determine how far my astral body is separated from my astral soul more accurately than the most respected professor.

HERWARTH!

I have composed (not written) my medical work, for which I certainly shall receive a doctoral cap, but may wear it only at Mardi Gras.

DEAR HERWARTH!

I have had an announcement placed in the *Berliner Tageblatt*, seeking the painter of *Simplicissimus*, Ludwig Kainer, and his wife, the painter. Both have suddenly disappeared. But sometimes I linger in their apartment. I ask myself what's going to happen to my various versions of myself?

LITTLE KURT!

Does one go to prison for saying 'bastard'? Or pay a fine? Or does a swearword, like, for example, 'son of a bitch,' come under a statute of limitations after two years? I called someone that two years ago; I would like to free myself from this chain.

I sometimes think of the dreamer of New Year's Eve at the Café des Westens. She knelt before me (a posture which I distinctly dislike), but she knelt in blood, because wine made an island of our table. I was wearing my war-dress and all my daggers, and I was never so distinguished a Prince of Thebes as on the threshold between the old and the new year. I had promised the dreamer to speak no more low German in my Norwegian correspondence; but basically the colloquial speech between me and Peter Boom is only an expression of brotherhood.

HERWARTH, KURT!

How do you find my likeness on the postage stamp issued by my city of Thebes? I shall love my people until my dying day.

DEAR HERWARTH!

You have no choice, I'm sending this letter to you until you publish it in *Der Sturm*. I believe you that printing these lines that come directly from my heart is painful for you, but because I have not learned to control myself, I demand it from you. For my sake you must tame polar bears – poodles are easier to train; once I said to you that most breeds only bark, groan, or yelp.

I was at *Everyman*, or is it called *All Kinds of Things*? I believe it is called *All Kinds of Things for Everyman* or *Everyman for All Kinds of Things*: Just step right in, gentlemen, to the giant Punch-and-Judy show, in the Berlin puppet-theater. We're putting on an evangelical play for 'baptized' Jews, very graphic and edifying. All baptized Jews had been at the evangelical show's performance/exhibition and were particularly edified by the blond Germanic angel in blue, with a double chin. On the right a little spot, a little spot on the left, human being or angel, on the Punch-and-Judy wall, and how the conscience began to howl: everyone here, everyone there. Where it came from – I think out of the stables, Herwarth. No, we would be better off to go to the Kermess in Cologne-on-the-Rhine, and visit a Cologne puppet theater, and there director Reinhardt should look for naiveté, and not have something manufactured from the Viennese style of Hofmannsthal or have a British evangelical mystery play whitewashed, with the even more terrible, boring, false rhyming of a play doctor. Just imagine, if he had become a sculptor, and had tinkered with the sculpture, replacing both arms of the Venus de Milo! Just look at the literature he dug up: first the *Oedipus* of Sophocles, and he fed it with Viennese blood; Electra he made into a demonic 'school-mistress'. He lacks imagination. People always say, Herwarth, because they become suspicious: 'So, haven't you yet read his poem, 'Children with big eyes?' I have even read his 'The Fool and Death' and 'The Death of Titian'; brilliant poems certainly, but carved in Goethe's granite. If Everyman knew what Everyman was, etc. – a blasphemy, a mockery of an ancient piety, of a religious composition. Life and death, sin and punishment, heaven and hell, everything is reduced to showmanship, like elephants and Arabian horses decorated with ribbons and knickknacks, but not like here, for the pleasure of children, but rather for the edification of the rich, pleasure-seeking public, damn it, to make the champagne taste better.

A few days before Christmas director Reinhardt asked for my play, *Die Wupper*. It's been lying in his house not quite two months; my play has life, my creatures want to go on living.

Now my play will be a hostage in Reinhardt's hands, he will throw my poetry into the fire, or have his secretary send it back to me with a few comments. All the same, I want to prevent the slightest indications of emotion or sentimentality, Herwarth, I must sacrifice my poetry to truth, in spite of 'ambition.' The Prince of Thebes casts off the last chain.

With a golden shovel I want to pave the way for the legend of my city or bury it, by telling the truth to director Reinhardt. The production of *Everyman* is inartistic and shameful – especially from a man whom the public thinks infallible, and who in truth cannot consciously blunder. How can one explain this cynicism? Does Reinhardt need money? Why don't his people rob for him: *They should rob the western part of the city for their emperor!!* Cashiers' drawers can't be deceived, but certainly audiences (there are able listeners among them) can be made dizzy by sleight of hand. Reinhardt should not permit himself such gifts. Outside the social democrats raged, it was election day – within me a stronger revolution raged, in the evening my last hope died that my play would be produced under the direction of Reinhardt, whom I had admired in so many of his productions. With this letter I demand the return of my tale of working people, the *Wupper*. Has he already read it? It must have impressed him.

DEAR BOTH OF YOU!

When I got up this morning a small sun was creeping on my foot, playfully darting in and out like a brilliantly colored lizard. I am very happy today, my room is sweet, the cold air that penetrates it tastes good and my wardrobe contains nothing but fine holiday dresses: one golden, one palm-colored, and a dress of crystal silk, which rustles. And my warrior outfits are peaceful, sweet borders of pearl adorn the wide black silk trousers, and from the shells of my belt snails encounter each other and stretch their little coral horns towards one another: *Allah machâh* – They are all shells that I picked up on the banks of the Nile. And in the pocket of my battle garb, among the hard shells of unripe fruit I find sugared roses that are sweet to eat. I am in love. –

LITTLE KURT, HERWARTH!

He says that he has broad hands. I find his hands wonderful and sweet, the small hands of a child, but seen through a magnifying glass, as though they definitely wanted to be big. I play all day with his hands; I have placed a ring on each finger, each bears a different rare stone. The one on his little finger tells the story of my great-grandfather, the sheik, the head priest of all mosques. On his ring-finger sits the myth of the fakir, the brother of the wife of the emir of Afghanistan, my mother's cousin. On his thumb the bloodiest war sits menacingly, a deeper stone with more fissures, with the picture of Constantine the crusader whose head I decapitated in the battle for Jerusalem. 'He' is himself a crusader, I find myself filled with amorous despair.

Will you both telegraph me whether it is tasteless for me to be in love with a knight?

Tino of Baghdad.

Instead of telegraphing your answer, you ask me who 'he' is. But I have already emphasized that I will say nothing more precise. He is tall and slender, and when his eyes open brightly they bloom like a field of corn flowers. I told him, each time he smiles as he opens his eyes, I'll give him a palace, or a golden palm tree, or a handful of black pearls or all of Asia. I must tell you something noteworthy: he begged me, tenderly urging me to comply, and on the following evening I didn't go to the café. On another evening I went back again; he was very sad, as he said, he had lost a battle. I'm troubled, he really should win every battle, even if I could help him by cutting off my head. Or do you think I might go to the café headless? Just with my torso, a dull stump, in the objective swamp! O, how pompous, no? But nothing brings you back to earth as the café does, after one has played the leading role in what one writes at the table at home. Delightful, to shake off one's most intense burden. Tell me, both of you, can the café harm me or not harm me? Herwarth, you always insist that I am a genius, it is your own business. Should I part from – 'him' – and return to the café, or should I stay with him? 'Come back, all is forgiven!' Damn! He has the most beautiful profile that I have ever seen, to whom should I confide this – to you, Herwarth: He is the Conrad whom I killed in Jerusalem, whom I hated in Jerusalem, together with all his crusaders in Jerusalem. In whom should I confide but you, Herwarth; the others are all Philistines. We are all purple, when we love we are gladioli, when we kiss he leads me into Asian heaven. We are no longer human. You never tell me anything, Herwarth, or I never let you get a word in, or don't you remember any longer that *we* are married?

I now have only him. But I am so eager to know how are things going at my home and my death stop, the Café des Westens? It is exactly as though I have lost an earring, I'm beginning to lose contact with myself. A drunkard needs his bar, a gambler his den, but I alone am not normal. But he means well, he says that people don't understand me. But the café is the only secret between us (he even knows you, Herwarth); the café lies like a coast between us. Is there now another place which contains such a bizarre-like array of colors as exist in our café?

DEAR HERWARTH, KURT!

Have you heard the latest? Caius-Maius has disappeared, he is no longer allowed to come into the café; they say that he has taken his own life, at least partially. I heard it myself in the café, I was disguised as a poet, only the collector of Kokoschka, Mr. Staub, recognized me, he is an oddball; it was yesterday, on the first spring day of February, the snow lay modestly on the field … I am a poetess!! But so many people came into the café, with so many strange animal faces, I wanted to have such a face just once, to strike fear in someone's heart. I would have liked to speak with the collector of Kokoschka; he also laughed once, but I would like to have – damn, if I knew what I wanted.

HERWARTH!

I have much to think about, I also am very fearful again. And I have such an odd feeling in my heart, I cannot sleep, and I dream realities with eyes wide open. There is a person in

Berlin who has the same heart that I have, your friend the doctor. His heart is checkered: yellow and orange colored with green dots. Gallows humor! And sometimes it is melancholy, then the churchyard mirrors itself in his pulse. That one must experience! But mine sometimes doubles in size, or becomes bluish purple. If he would at least experience the rapture of his heart; but sometimes he feels restlessness. I know all kinds of hearts, but not that of the bourgeois. O the fear in the heart when the heart sinks into a crater of water or is suspended between earth and sky in the teeth of the moon, or it sinks – O the moment when my city Thebes-Bagdhad sinks. Look at the picture, Herwarth, how clearly all things and not-things of the heart are drawn. Shouldn't one believe in reality, can it be rejected? Is this little section on the heart's feelings of my medicinal poetry worth including?

Farewell, I still want to write to the Dalai Lama.

VERY HONORED DALAI-LAMA

I shall rattle on the red door of your *Fackel* until you open it for me. I have a new poem, I have composed a new poem. I insist that it appear in your *Fackel*, come hell or high water, it must be published in your journal. Whether or not you are writing it alone, I don't care – it must be. Your *Fackel* is my red garden, I carried your *Fackel* like a rose above my heart, your *Fackel* is my rosy-red prospect, my red bread-winner. You do not have the right to write *Die Fackel* alone, how can I get enough red to continue nourishing myself?

Greetings to you, sir, from the Prince of Thebes and his black servants Ossman and Tecofi, the chief's son.

Soon there will be nothing left to say, Herwarth and Kurt. By the way, you have been back in Berlin again quite a while, and my Norwegian letters are coming to an end. It seems to me that soon I'll have nothing more to say; who will go on speaking my poems? Only Prince Antony of Poland knows how to speak them, his moonlight voice is transparent, and all the listening visions will be mirrored in my poems. Soon it will be impossible for me to live among people: I am extremely bored, it is beyond expression, I see no end to it, and do not know where the boredom and sadness may end. He, the prince, speaks my poems, in a way that makes them illuminate all paths, for all those moving towards the blue or towards the unknown.

UNBELIEVABLE, HERWARTH!

I believe finally that it's all up with me, because the German poet Hans Ehrenbaum-Degele has challenged me to a duel. On behalf of German myth and lofty song. His second will be the actor Wilhelm Murnau, and a quack to take care of wounds will be present. But to urge me on, my black Tecofi-Folifi Temanu will perform his dance of human bones during the fight.

TELEGRAM:

Herwarth Walden, Halensee, Katharinenstrasse 5.

My right hand cut to the quick by a rapier!

DEAR HERWARTH!

I have brought great disgrace upon my city Thebes. For a warrior it is shameful to be sick, but for me it is an irremediable disgrace to lie wounded in the tent, wounded by an Occidental victor. Both my black servants are howling like women, creeping about the house like cunning cats under a full moon; I am in a bad mood.

The Prince.

Yesterday I shut myself up in the private room of my palace and prayed. I had almost forgotten how to say prayers, which are carved like harps. Absorbed in thought, I kissed my mother's feet; how pious one can become, I was at that moment of golden humility without sin. You think that there are no sins, but I no longer doubt that, because I am still praying and am bleached by the pious kiss. Should I open my heart?

HERWARTH!

How one never finds oneself! That always indirectly has a cosmic reason. I move restlessly from star to star; if I were not Lucifer's sister I would be the eternal angel. At the moment you stand exactly, as calculated by the observatory, at the tropic of the warring *Sturm*-cock. Bravo!

DEAR HERWARTH!

This evening I sat on the roof and looked down, with the moon, on Thebes; but I fell asleep and dreamed that my strongest battleship had filled with water and sunk. Then I thought of you – if ever a loose woman got hold of you! For water, whether a brook or a pond, a river or an ocean, conceals in itself the sinuous, tempting guts of a woman. No ship is safe from her. – *I can't stand you anymore.*

DEAR HERWARTH!

I have drawn Richard Dehmel, I have drawn him blood red, as an oriental city-scape; not in the frock coat with which he customarily meets the outside world, but in the old-fashioned city-turban. Richard Dehmel's poems flow like blood, each one a blood-letting and a transfusion at the same time. He is the grand calif of all poetry.

YOU TWO FRIENDS!

What's going on here? Were you already waiting there, at the corner of Kurfürstendamm and Wilmersdorferstrasse, in the Café Kurfürstendamm? God, I have become disloyal to the Café des Westens; how I have abandoned the coffee house, like a beloved to whom I pledged eternal loyalty. The

Café Kurfürstendamm is a woman, an Asian dancer. She amuses me, consoles me, charms me with the many sweet colors of her clothing. There is movement in the café, it twists mysteriously, like the gleaming body of Fatima. The small recesses of the galleries, covered with stars, are veiled hearts. O, the things one can say and hear there – violins quietly singing, blissful moods. The café is the embodiment of Lucien Bernard's poster. I shall have the order of the crescent moon bestowed upon him as a sign of my respectful admiration, appointing him pasha of Thebes.

HERWARTH, LITTLE KURT!

Today I myself am writing the 'unwritten' lines to Sascha in the citadel in Russia. Don't have my flaming myrtle letter published.

TELEGRAM:

Just elected reigning Prince in Thebes. Long live the capital and my people!

They are waiting for me in my city, costly rugs hang from the roofs down to the ground. They unwind and rewind again. Since sunrise my Negroes have been lying before me on their black bellies, and in the evening will go among the people, teaching the word 'highness,' until the word dances in their mouths. I am highness. Note this, emphasize this to everyone you come across. But this honor gives me pain, for I cannot return to my city, I have no money. And eastern countries love splendor; they seize stars from the clouds, and they store up in their hearts the golden wheat of the sky. Here there are no stars, small scattered grains glitter as they fall to the ground. O, how poor this eastern land, here no paradise grows, no angel, no miracle.

How this poverty has made me ashamed, your poverty; even my damask-skin is gone; my miserable feet are torn to pieces – I look down upon my own highness with scorn. But the Negroes have delicate feelings; they have invented a game, we are already rehearsing the roles of the people and the king. They congregate in droves on both sides of me, hundreds of thousands or millions of turbaned heads, yelling and screaming, *Allah machâh!* And they applaud – I smile and waft gracious kisses among the people. I am dresssed all in gold, like the full moon, my hair glitters, the nails of my fingers are pearls; I am carried into the palace and I give to my dear people a constitution.

I hope that my letters have not bored you, or has little Kurt yawned often? Read my letter once again, Herwarth, the one that ends with: 'I am the life'. How proud! Now I am a transparent, bottomless ocean, I feel that there is no solid ground beneath me any longer. You should not have wavered, Herwarth. What good to me now are your ready and willing hands, and all the other clutching, anxious fingers surrounding me, through which my boundless soul flows. Soon death will inundate everything, everything is blurred in me, my thoughts and feelings. I have never made a system, the way wise women do, never buttressed myself with a world-view, the way even wiser men do, I have not built an ark. I have no focus, my words are spread out everywhere, my words came from everywhere; I received and turned inward, thus I was always the reigning Prince of Thebes. How old am I, Herwarth? One thousand and fourteen. A petit bourgeois never reaches one thousand and fourteen, but sometimes reaches one hundred and fourteen, if he has good intentions. Herwarth, have you been faithful to me? For the sake of good taste, in your own interest, I would prefer to think that you were faithful to me. Do not use me as a model by which to judge yourself; I have never felt that people were more than a frame in which I placed myself; sometimes, frankly speaking, I lost myself in them; two were golden, Herwarth, to one of whom my heart was devoted. It is wonderful to be in love, so intoxicating, so overpowering, so irresponsible, the heart is always dizzy; yesterday I stood before the picture of the proud Medici, he came back to life and wanted to carry me away in the night. How bourgeois is love in comparison to being in love; someone must have loved me. Did you love me, Herwarth? Who has loved me?

I would throw myself at his feet at this moment, as though I were in front of a rock, before a precious altar, I, the Prince of Thebes. I would carry the beloved with me in death, as the Egyptian kings carried their treasures, their golden pitchers with them into their tombs and contemptuously drank the last remnants out of them. I flee into the thicket, Herwarth, I have always hated the house, even the palace itself; just call a room property and you are already domesticated. I hate domesticity, therefore hate the last confinement, the tomb. I move into the deepest forest, Herwarth; what I do is well done, I have no doubts about myself. Can one make a more believable statement without provoking a smile? Or is there a grasshopper hopping somewhere? I lie down under big trees and stretch myself out along their roots, entwined with each other like gnarled snakes. I no longer hear in my ears the sound of little bells; every beat of my heart was a dance. I can no longer dance, Herwarth; I cry – snow falls on my weeping eyes. Hello, Greek Thebes, my city, do not forget the prophet saint Peter Hille the way you forgot me; he wrote prophetically: my world is shattered. I rise up once again, sink my wild daggers in the earth, a crown of victory for my head. Here and no further!

END

Olvenstedt bei Magdeburg

D.H.!

This morning, when I took your travel-bag from the trunk, Herwarth, an unpublished letter from me was stuck inside it, which I once sent to you and little Kurt in Norway – with my self-portrait wrapped in silk paper; this is definitely stealing from art historians. For I have made no sketch of myself, also no painting, I have placed a mere creature on paper. I shall quickly send you the lost lines and my enormously valuable self-portrait. At most it costs five or six marks to make a plate of it. Give up two evenings at the café, offer a sacrifice to my picture. I have placed the chest with my love letters under my bed, to give you something to do. Meanwhile I am resting here in the country; I go for walks with Richard Fuchs and Otto Fuchs, through their greenhouses, and watch the carnations grow. But it is terribly cold and the rustling trees are enough to drive you crazy. I'm going to cut them down tonight, damn it!

Greetings to you, your E.

DEAR AMBASSADORS!

When you are in Berlin again, I probably shall be in Thebes, at the dedication of my bas-relief on the wall. But I am not anxious to see myself, since I have never recognized myself, either in sculpture or in painting, or even in cast. In my portrait I look for the changing play of day and night, sleep and waking. Doesn't my mouth in my self-portrait emit a call to battle? An Egyptian arabesque, a royal hieroglyph, my nose; my hair darting like arrows, and my neck carries its head powerfully. In this manner I give myself to the people of my city. Ossman and Tecofi Temanu, my black servants, will carry my self-portrait on a banner through the streets of Thebes. So my people will celebrate me, so I celebrate myself.

Your Prince of Thebes.

INFIDELS

My people always wish to see my face, hear my voice.

Under the early morning star named after me, I speak to my city and open my soul to her people like a grove of palms they may enter.

The sky is my mirror.

My portrait is being distributed in Thebes.

JUSSUF – PRINCE

GLOSSARY

ACHED BEY, Reference to the tale of the same name in Else
  Lasker-Schüler's prose work *Die Nächte Tino von Bagdads*
  (1907).
ALLAH MACHÂH, Variation on the Arabic 'masha'Allah', a
  phrase expressing surprise, joy or gratitude.
ALTENBERG, Peter (1859-1919), Real name: Richard
  Engländer; Viennese writer; friend of Karl Kraus and Kete
  Parsenow.
AMANDA WALLBRECKER, Name of a character in Else Lasker-
  Schüler's play *Die Wupper*.
ANTONI, THE PRINCE OF POLAND, Unidentified.

BARRISON, Gertrude (1880-1946), Danish-American
  dancer; famous as one of the risqué Five Sisters Barrison
  dance troupe, first in Germany, later in Vienna, where she
  befriended Karl Kraus and Peter Altenberg.
BAUM, Peter (1869-1916), German poet and writer; friend
  of Peter Hille; contributor to *Der Sturm*.
BERLIN SECESSION. Artists' collective founded in 1898. The
  painter Max Liebermann was its most prominent member.

BERLINER TAGEBLATT, Democratic German daily published from 1848.

BERNARD, Lucien (1883-1972), German interior designer and graphic artist.

BERNCASTLE DOKTOR, i.e. the Bernkasteler Doktor, a vineyard in Germany's Mosel valley famous for its Riesling wines.

BERNEIS, Benno (1884-1916), Painter; member of the Berlin Secession.

BISHOP, See: Kurt Hiller.

BLASS, Ernst (1890-1939), Expressionist poet and writer; co-founder of the Neuen Club.

BOLLE, Dairy company in Berlin.

CAFÉ AUSTRIA, See: Gnu.

CAFÉ DES WESTENS, The café on the corner of Kurfürstendamm and Joachimstalerstrasse that was the central meeting place for artists and writers of the pre-WWI decade; it closed in 1915. Referred to as 'the café' throughout much of the text.

CAIUS-MAIUS, See: Kurt Hiller.

CARO, Dr. Hugo (?-1918), Public prosecutor in Berlin.

CARO, Jeptha Elfriede, Wife of Hugo Caro.

CASSIRER, Paul (1871-1926), Gallerist and publisher who would publish Else Lasker-Schüler's collected works in 1919 and 1920; owned the gallery Kunstsalon Cassirer on Victoriastrasse 35 in Berlin together with his cousin Bruno Cassirer.

'CHILDREN WITH BIG EYES … TITIAN' (p. 84), reference to various poems and works by Hugo von Hofmannsthal.

CHORALION HALL, Former concert hall in Berlin's Bellevuestrasse.

Cohn, Professor, i.e. Siegbert Cohn; one half of Oesterheld und Cohn, who published Else Lasker-Schüler's play *Die Wupper* in 1919.

Cook and Peary, Reference to the American arctic explorers Fredric Cook and Robert Edwin Peary, both of whom claimed to be the first to have reached the North Pole around 1909.

Count of Luxemburg, reference to the operetta of the same name by Franz Lehár (1909).

Croesus, King of Lydia from 560-546 BC.

Dalai Lama (in Vienna), i.e. Karl Kraus.

Daniel Jesus, Name of the protagonist of Paul Leppin's novel of the same name (1905).

Dehmel, Richard (1863-1920), German Poet and playwright.

Destinn, Emmy (1878-1930), Czech opera singer.

Deutschen Theater, Theater in Berlin's Mitte district founded in 1850, currently known as the Theater am Schiffbauerdamm.

D.H.!, i.e. Dear Herwarth!

Döblin, Alfred/Doctor Döblin (1878-1957), German writer and doctor, who worked in the hospital on Urbanstrasse, Berlin Kreuzberg; author of *Berlin Alexanderplatz* (1929).

Don't tell me about Rome, Quotation from Richard Wagner's *Tannhäuser*.

Durieux, Tilla (1880-1971), Real name: Ottillie Godeffroy; Austrian theatre and film actress who worked with Max Reinhardt, Jakob van Hoddis and Kurt Hiller as part of the Neuen Club; married to Paul Cassirer.

EGYPTIAN EXHIBITION, So-called anthropological or ethnological 'Völkerschauen' event in the Luna Park, featuring Egyptian-themed streets, scenes and people, where events were organized such as staged weddings and dances.

EHRENBAUM-DEGELE, Hans (1880-1950), Poet and playwright; performed in the Gnu cabaret; died in WWI.

EHRENSTEIN, Albert (1886-1950), Viennese author of the novella *Tubutsch*, which was serialized in *Der Sturm* more or less simultaneously with the letters of *My Heart*; friend of Oskar Kokoschka; moved to New York in 1941.

ELBERFELD, Former town near Wuppertal that has currently become part of the city.

EVERYMAN, i.e. Hugo von Hofmannsthal's play *Jedermann* (1911).

FACHINGER, Brand of mineral water.

FACKEL, The journal published by Karl Kraus between 1899 and 1936; known for its red cover.

FREUNDLICH, Otto (1878-1943), German abstract painter and sculptor; featured in Walden's Sturm gallery and in several exhibitions of the Berlin Secession.

FRIEDLÄNDER, Regina, Famous hat designer in Berlin.

FRIEDRICHSTRASSE, Major street in Berlin's Mitte district.

FRIEDRICHSRUHERPETERBAUMSTRASSE, Variation on Friedrichsruherstrasse, the street in Berlin where Peter Baum lived.

FRÖHLICH, Max, German painter; contributor to *Der Sturm*; designed the cover of Else Lasker-Schüler's 1907 prose collection *Die Nächte Tino von Bagdads*.

FUCHS, Richard (??-1972), Worked for *Der Sturm*.

FÜRST-FOERSTER, Auguste (??-1912), A friend of Else Lasker-Schüler.

GANGOLF, Paul (1879-1936), Real name: Paul Loewy; painter and graphic artist; friend of Peter Hille; contributor to *Der Sturm*.

GARTENLAUBE, Illustrated weekly from Leipzig.

GEGENWART, Berlin weekly for literature and the arts (1872-1931).

GEORGE, Stefan (1868-1933), German poet and writer.

GERSON, Department store in Berlin.

GNU, Literary cabaret founded in 1911 by Kurt Hiller and Ernst Blass, events were held in the Café Austria on Berlin's Potsdammerstrasse 28.

GOLO GANGES (or: Golo Gangi), Pseudonym of Erwin Loewenson (1880-1963), writer; member of the Neuen Club.

GRÄTZ, i.e. Paul Graetz (1890-1937), German-Jewish comic and actor for theater and film who starred in several roles under the direction of Max Reinhardt at the Deutschen Theater. In this passage (p. 13) the text variation of the second (1920) edition of *My Heart* has been retained rather than that which appeared in the original *Sturm* version, where, instead of 'Grätz', the actor was named as Rudolf Blümner, the play given the title *Pastor Kraatz* and the director remained anonymous. When Reinhardt eventually staged *Die Wupper* in 1919, the 'old grandfather' was indeed played by Graetz.

GROßE ROSINEN, Farce by Rudolf Bernauer which premiered in the Berliner Theater on 31 December 1911.

GUHLKE, Fridolin, Caricaturist for *Der Sturm*.

HAAS, Willy (1891-1973), Literary critic from Prague. Also see: Willy Himmel.

HALENSEE, District in Berlin.

HARDT, Ludwig (1886-1947), German theater and film actor.

HART, Julius (1859-1930), Poet and founding member of the Neue Gemeinschaft.

HAUPTMANN, Gerhart (1862-1946), German writer and dramatist.

HELLMUTH, Martha (1854-??), German writer.

HENRIETTENPLATZ, Square in Berlin's Halensee district.

HERRMANN, Max (1865-1942), Literary and theater historian; professor of philology.

HERWARTH, See: Herwarth Walden.

HIDDENSEE, German island in the Baltic Sea.

HILLE, Peter (1854-1904), Writer; the central figure of the Neue Gemeinschaft; Saint Peter in Else Lasker-Schüler's *Das Peter Hille-Buch* (1906).

HILLER, Kurt (1885-1972), Writer, co-founder of the Neuen Club, the Neopathetic Cabaret and the Gnu cabaret; contributor to *Der Sturm*.

HIMMEL, Willy, In the book publication of *Mein Herz* (1909) he is identified Wilhelm Haas.

HIS NOVEL OF THE ROCOCO PERIOD (p. 11), i.e. Peter Baum's *Kammermusik. Ein Rokokoroman*, 1914.

HODDIS, Jakob van (1887-1942), real name: Hans Davidssohn; poet and co-founder of the Neuen Club.

HOFMANNSTHAL, Hugo von (1874-1929), Austrian writer.

HOHENZOLLERNDAMM, street in Berlin's Wilmersdorf district.

HÖXTER, John (1884-1938), Painter and writer; founder of the Dadaist journal *Der blutige Ernst*; member of the Neopathetic Cabaret.

HUBERT, Ali (1878-1940), Austrian painter and costume designer.

JAKOBSOHN, i.e. Siegfried Jacobsohn (1881-1926), German publicist and theatre critic.

JULIUS LIEBAN … MAUPASSANT (p. 23), All these are people on whom Else Lasker-Schüler had published essays or reviews in *Der Sturm* and other journals.

KAINER, LENE, Wife of Ludwig Kainer.

KAINER, LUDWIG (1885-1967), painter and graphic artist; contributor to *Simplicissimus*.

KARL VON MOOR, Character from Schiller's famous play *Die Räuber*.

KEMPINSKI, Famous restaurant in Berlin's Leipzigerstrasse 25.

KLEIST, Heinrich von (1777-1811), German poet, dramatist and novelist, after whom the prestigious Kleist Prize for literature is named.

KNIE-GÖRLITZER, 'The underground allude to here, was actually represented as an earth-coloured line on contemporary network maps, and it did have a station bearing the suggestive name *Knie* [i.e. 'knee'] (today's Ernst-Reuter-Platz) indicating a bend in the line.' Quoted from Andreas Kramer, "The Traffic of Gender in Expressionist Prose Writing", in: *Expressionism and Gender*, ed. by Frank Krause (Goettingen: V&R unipress, 2010), p.57. The Knie station, opened in 1902, was the western terminus of Berlin's first U-Bahn track, which connected

Charlottenberg, via the Görlitzer station in Kreuzberg, to the Friedrichshain district across the river Spree.

KNOBLAUCH, Adolf (1882-1951), Writer, translator and publisher.

KOCH, Georg (1885-??), Sculptor who exhibited with the Berlin Secession.

KOKOSCHKA, Oskar (1886-1980), Austrian painter, poet and playwright.

KRANZLER, coffeehouse on Berlin's Unter den Linden.

KRAUS, Karl (1874-1936), Viennese writer, satirist and publisher of *Die Fackel*; author of *The Last Days of Mankind*; Friend of Herwarth Walden and Else Lasker-Schüler, whose house on Katharinenstrasse 5 served as the Berlin office of *Die Fackel* between 1909 and 1911; Kraus financially supported the publication of *Der Sturm* between 1909-1912.

KRÖGEL, An old run down street in Berlin, broken down in 1935.

KRUMMACHER, Pastor Friedrich Wilhelm (1796-1868), Reformed pastor from Eberfeld.

KURFÜRSTENDAMM, Main boulevard in Berlin's West-End district.

KURT, i.e Kurt Neimann (1877-1944), Attorney and friend of Herwarth Walden.

KURTZ, Rudolf (1884-1960), Writer and film director; contributor to *Der Sturm*.

LANTZ, Adolf (1882-??), Theater director in Berlin; journalist.

LEDERER, Fritz (1878-1949), German landscape painter and graphic artist.

LEPPIN, Paul (1878-1945), writer from Prague. See: Daniel Jesus.

'LET US SPEAK AGAIN OF LOVE, AS ONCE IN MAY', line from the poem "Allerseelen" set to music by Richard Strauss.

LILIENCRON, Detlev von (1844-1909), German writer and poet.

LOOS, Adolf (1870-1933), Austrian modernist architect; friend of Karl Kraus.

LUBINSKI, Samuel (1868-1910), Writer, literary historian, philosopher of religion.

LUDWIG CRANACH, i.e. Lucas Cranach The Elder (1472-135), German Renaissance painter.

LUNA PARK, Large amusement park on the shore of Berlin's Halensee lake which opened in 1909, featuring a fairy tale castle and towers, fairground attractions and all manner of entertainment in the form of jazz nights, cabaret, boxing matches etc., as well as 'anthropological shows' such as the Egyptian Exhibition; it closed 1933.

MANN, Heinrich (1871-1950), German writer; author of the novel *Professor Unrat* (1905), which would be adapted for the screen as *Der blaue Engel*, starring Marlene Dietrich (1930).

MEINHARD, Carl (1875-1949), Director of the Berliner Theater.

MICHAELIS, Karin (1872-1950), Danish author and journalist.

MINN, Else Lasker-Schüler refers to the character of the same name in her prose work *Die Nächte Tino von Bagdads* (1907).

Mohammed Pasha ... Fakir (p. 70), These are characters
that also feature in *Die Nächte Tino von Bagdads*.

Mommenstrasse, Street in Berlin's Charlottenburg district.

Mouse Tower outside Bingen, According to legend the
particularly cold-hearted archbishop Hatto II was eaten
alive by mice in this tower.

Mr. Barchan, the sorcerer, i.e. Paul Barchan, writer whose
translation of a prose text by Tschechow was published
in *Die Fackel*, which led to a conflict when Karl Kraus
discovered it was not, as professed, the first translation of
the text to appear. Kraus took him to task in the next issue
of *Die Fackel*, copies of which Barchan then tried to 'make
disappear' from the café.

Murnau, Friedrich Wilhelm (1888-1931), Film actor and
director, notably of the Expressionist masterpiece *Nosferatu*
(1922).

My Arabian book (p. 3), i.e. *Die Nächte Tino von Bagdads*
(1907)

My Calif-stories (p. 70), either *Die Nächte Tino von
Bagdads* or *Der Prinz von Theben*.

My fakir (p. 25), Character from a tale of the same name in
her *Der Prinz von Theben* (1908).

My old Tibetan tapestry (p. 80), referring to her poem
"Ein alter Tibetteppich" (1906).

My Paul (p. 25), i.e. Paul Lasker-Schüler (1899-1927),
The son of Else Lasker-Schüler.

My uncle (p. 78), the southern minister, i.e. Leopold
Sonnemann (1831-1909), journalist, publisher and
editor of the *Frankfurter Zeitung*, founder of the German
People's Party.

NEUE GEMEINSCHAFT, Anarchist/communist artists' commune on the outskirts of Berlin established by Julius Hart in 1909, with Peter Hille as its central figure. Among its members: Else Lasker-Schüler, Erich Mühsam, Rudolf Steiner and Martin Buber.

NEUEN CLUB, Artists' and students' collective founded in 1909 by Kurt Hiller and Jakob van Hoddis which functioned as the nucleus of literary Expressionism.

NEW SECESSION, Expressionist artists' collective that separated itself from the older Berlin Secession in 1910. Max Pechstein was its unofficial leader.

NOLDE, Emil (1867-1956), German-Danish painter; member of the Expressionist artists' collective Die Brücke.

OESTERHELD, Erich (1883-1920), One half of Oesterheld und Cohn, who published Else Lasker-Schüler's play *Die Wupper* in 1919.

OPPENHEIMER, Max (1885-1954), Austrian painter, a.k.a. Mopp; on several occasions when Oppenheimer exhibited his work, in München in May 1911 and in Berlin in 1912, this provoked Oskar Kokoschka to protest and accuse Oppenheimer of plagiarism, a claim supported by Karl Kraus, Herwarth Walden and Else Lasker-Schüler.

PAINTED ME SITTING IN A TENT (p. 74), the painting in question is arguably Schmidt-Rottluff's "Lesende" ['Reader'] of 1912.

PAN, Literary and art periodical published by Paul Cassirer.

PARSENOW, Kete (1880-1960), Actress; wife of Walter Friedrich Otto; the 'Venus of Siam'.

PECHSTEIN, Max (1881-1955), Painter and member of the Expressionist artists' collective *Die Brücke*.

PETER BOOM, See: Peter Baum.

PINSKY, Chamay, Writer and contributor to *Der Sturm*.

PITTER, i.e. Peter Baum.

POIRET, Paul (1879-1944), French fashion designer known for his orientalist style.

POTSDAMMERSTRASSE, Street connecting Berlin's Tiergarten and Schöneberg districts.

PRATER, Park in Vienna; site of the Wurstelprater amusement park famous for its Ferris wheel.

PRINCE OF THEBES, Poetic alter ego, used here for the first time, which will reappear in *Der Prinz von Theben*, a collection of nine tales, with drawings by the author and Franz Marc, published in 1914.

RAMSENITH, a variation of the Egyptian pharaonic name Ramses.

RATTKE, waiter in Café des Westens.

REINHARDT, Max (1873-1943), Influential Austrian actor and film and theater director.

REISS, Erna, i.e. Erna Charlotte Döblin; wife of Alfred Döblin.

RHEINGOLD, Former restaurant in Berlin's Tiergarten district.

RICHTER, M., Probably Max Richter (1860-?), landscape painter and illustrator.

RINGBAHNSTRASSE, Street in Berlin Schöneberg district.

RÜBEZAHL, Figure from German folklore.

RUBINSTEIN, Anton (1829-1894), Russian composer.

SCHENNIS, Friedrich von (1852-1918), Landscape painter.

SCHERL, August (1849-1921), Publisher of newspapers and journals.

SCHMIDT-ROTTLUFF, Karl (1884-1976), Painter and member of the Expressionist artists' collective Die Brücke.

SCHÖNBERG, Arnold (1874-1951), Austrian composer and painter.

SIMPLICISSIMUS, Satirical magazine from Munich, 1896-1976.

SPELA, MRS., i.e. Spela Albrecht, German-Russian chansonnière.

STIVARIUS, Matja, Pianist; member of the Neuen Gemeinschaft; wife of Peter Baum.

STURM, The journal for Expressionist and Modernist art and literature founded by Herwarth Walden in 1910.

TECOFI, i.e. Tecofi Temanu; apparently the name of an African student living in Berlin at the time.

TIERGARTENSTRASSE, Street in Berlin's Tiergarten district.

TILL EULENSPIEGEL, Trickster figure from German folklore.

TINO OF BAGHDAD, Poetic alter-ego of Else Lasker-Schüler which appeared earlier as the narrator in *Das Peter Hille-Buch* (1906) and as the protagonist of *Die Nächte Tino von Bagdads* (1907).

TRAPP, Hede von (1877-1947), Austrian poet, painter and graphic designer.

TRISTAN, See: Ehrenbaum-Degele, Hans.

ULLMAN, Ludwig (1887-1959), theatermaker, writer and publisher; worked as secretary for Karl Kraus and *Die Fackel*.

VENUS OF SIAM, See: Kete Parsenow.

VORWÄRTS, publication of the German social democratic party.

Voss, i.e. the newspaper *Vossische Zeitung*.

WALDEN, Herwarth (1878-1941), Real name: Georg Levin; writer and composer; publisher of the journal *Der Sturm* (1910-1932) and founder of the Sturm publishing house and gallery, all of which championed Expressionist and Modernist art and literature; married to Else Lasker-Schüler from 1903-1912.

WALLBRECKER, Amanda, See: Amanda.

WAUER, Director/William (1866-1962), Sculptor, painter and theater-director; contributor to *Der Sturm*.

WEISS, Richard, Austrian poet.

WILMERSDORFERSTRASSE, Street in Berlin's Wilmersdorf district.

WINTERGARTEN, Famous cabaret In Berlin's Friedrichstrasse.

WÜLLNER, Ludwig (188-1938), Actor and singer.

WUPPER, i.e. *Die Wupper*; play in five acts by Else Lasker-Schüler; published 1909 and staged 1919.

WUPPERTAL, City in North Rhine-Westphalia, Germany.

YOUR PANTOMIME (pp. 14, 15), i.e. *Die vier Toten der Fiametta*, pantomime by William Wauer with music composed by Herwarth Walden (1911).

ZECH, Paul (1881-1946), German writer and publisher.

ZEUXIS, Greek painter of the 5th century BC; see: Oskar Kokoschka.

In compiling the glossary frequent use has been made of the information contained in the excellent German edition of *Mein Herz* edited by Ricarda Dick (Jüdischer Verlag, 2003), and in the *Marzbacher Magazin* issue 'Else Lasker-Schüler 1869-1945' edited by Erika Klüsener and Friedrich Pfäfflin (issue 71, 1995).

PUBLISHER'S NOTE

This translation is based on the original text of the *Briefe nach Norwegen* [Letters to Norway] published in *Der Sturm* between September 1911 and February 1912. When these letters appeared in book-form under the title *Mein Herz* later in 1912, the names of several characters had been changed to conceal the identity of the people on whom they were modelled. These variations are listed in the glossary of the present edition. The 'pictures' (drawings by Else Lasker-Schüler) mentioned in the book's subtitle are not reproduced here. The dedication to Adolf Loos stems from the 1912 edition; in the second, 1920, edition this was replaced by the phrase 'Mein Herz – Niemandem', i.e. 'My heart – belongs to no one'.

Printed in Great Britain
by Amazon

45931094R00081